CUPHEAD

~COMIC CAPERS & CURIOS~

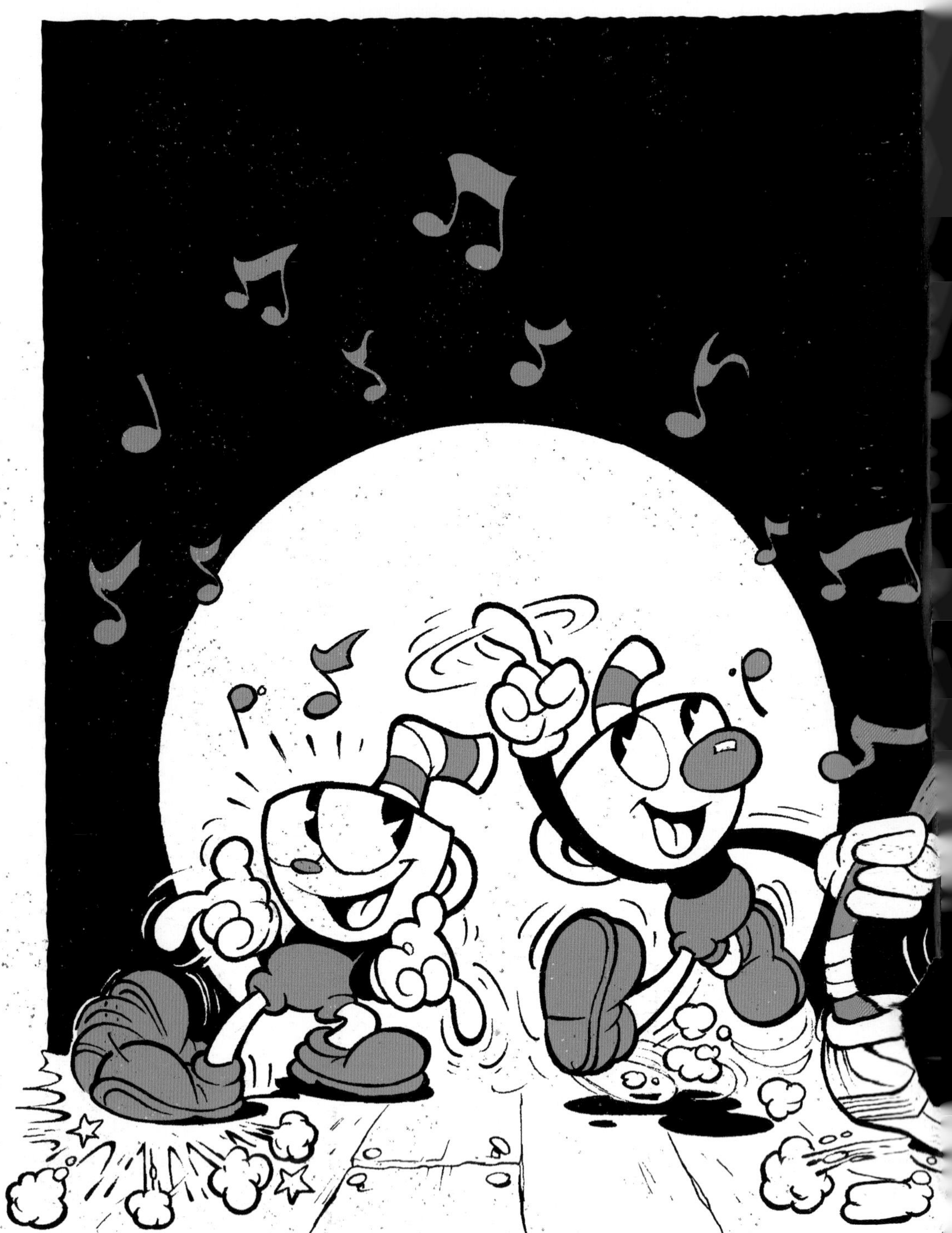

CUPHEAD
COMIC CAPERS & CURIOS

WRITTEN BY
ZACK KELLER

ART, LETTERS & COVER BY
SHAWN DICKINSON

COLORS BY
KRISTINA LUU

DARK HORSE BOOKS

PRESIDENT AND PUBLISHER
MIKE RICHARDSON

EDITOR
MEGAN WALKER

ASSISTANT EDITOR
JOSHUA ENGLEDOW

DESIGNER
ETHAN KIMBERLING

DIGITAL ART TECHNICIAN
ALLYSON HALLER

SPECIAL THANKS TO
IAN CLARKE, ELI CYMET, TYLER MOLDENHAUER, AND THE ENTIRE STUDIO MDHR TEAM

CUPHEAD VOLUME 1: COMIC CAPERS & CURIOS

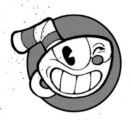

Published by Dark Horse Books
A division of Dark Horse Comics LLC
10956 SE Main Street
Milwaukie, OR 97222

DarkHorse.com

Facebook.com/DarkHorseComics
Twitter.com/DarkHorseComics

Advertising Sales: (503) 905-2315
To find a comics shop in your area, visit comicshoplocator.com

First Edition: July 2020
Ebook ISBN 978-1-50671-297-0
Trade Paperback ISBN 978-1-50671-248-2
3 5 7 9 10 8 6 4 2
Printed in China

Library of Congress Cataloging-in-Publication Data

Names: Keller, Zack, writer. | Dickinson, Shawn, 1980- artist. | Luu, Kristina, colourist.
Title: Comic capers & curios / written by Zack Keller ; art, letters & cover by Shawn Dickinson ; colors by Kristina Luu.
Other titles: Comic capers and curios
Description: First edition. | Milwaukie, OR : Dark Horse Books, 2020. | Series: Cuphead vol. 1 | Summary: "Revisit the colorful characters of the Inkwell Isles in this collection of brand new Cuphead and Mugman tales! Prone to unexpected predicaments and thrilling adventures, Cuphead and Mugman feature front and center in a series of short but sweet side stories that reimagine the world of the all-cartoon magical wondergame. This original graphic novel features all-new original tales, authentically drawn to match the glorious, award-winning vintage animation style of Cuphead!"-- Provided by publisher.
Identifiers: LCCN 2019060068 | ISBN 9781506712482 (trade paperback) | ISBN 9781506712970 (ebook)
Subjects: LCSH: Comic books, strips, etc.
Classification: LCC PN6728.C828 K45 2020 | DDC 741.5/973--dc23
LC record available at https://lccn.loc.gov/2019060068

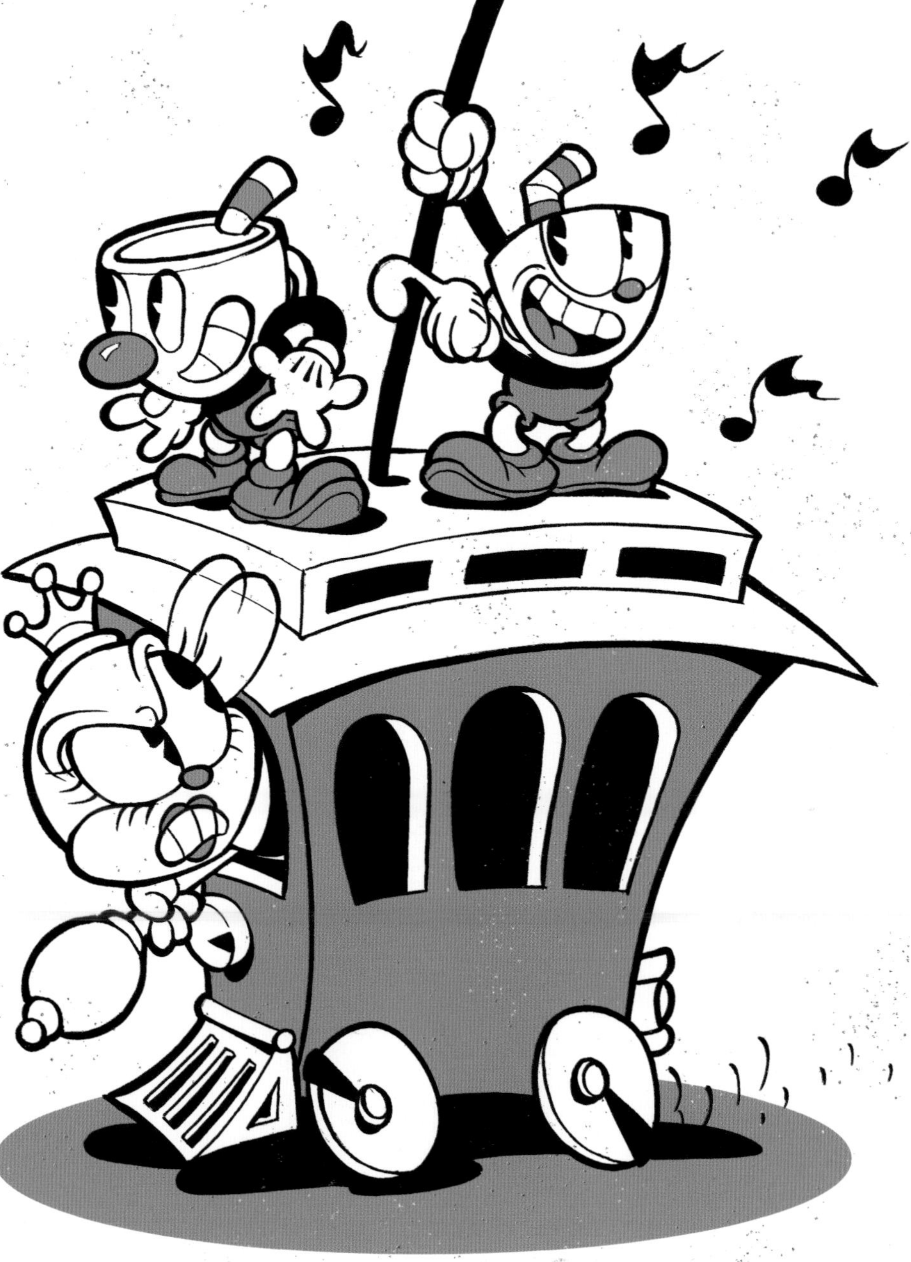

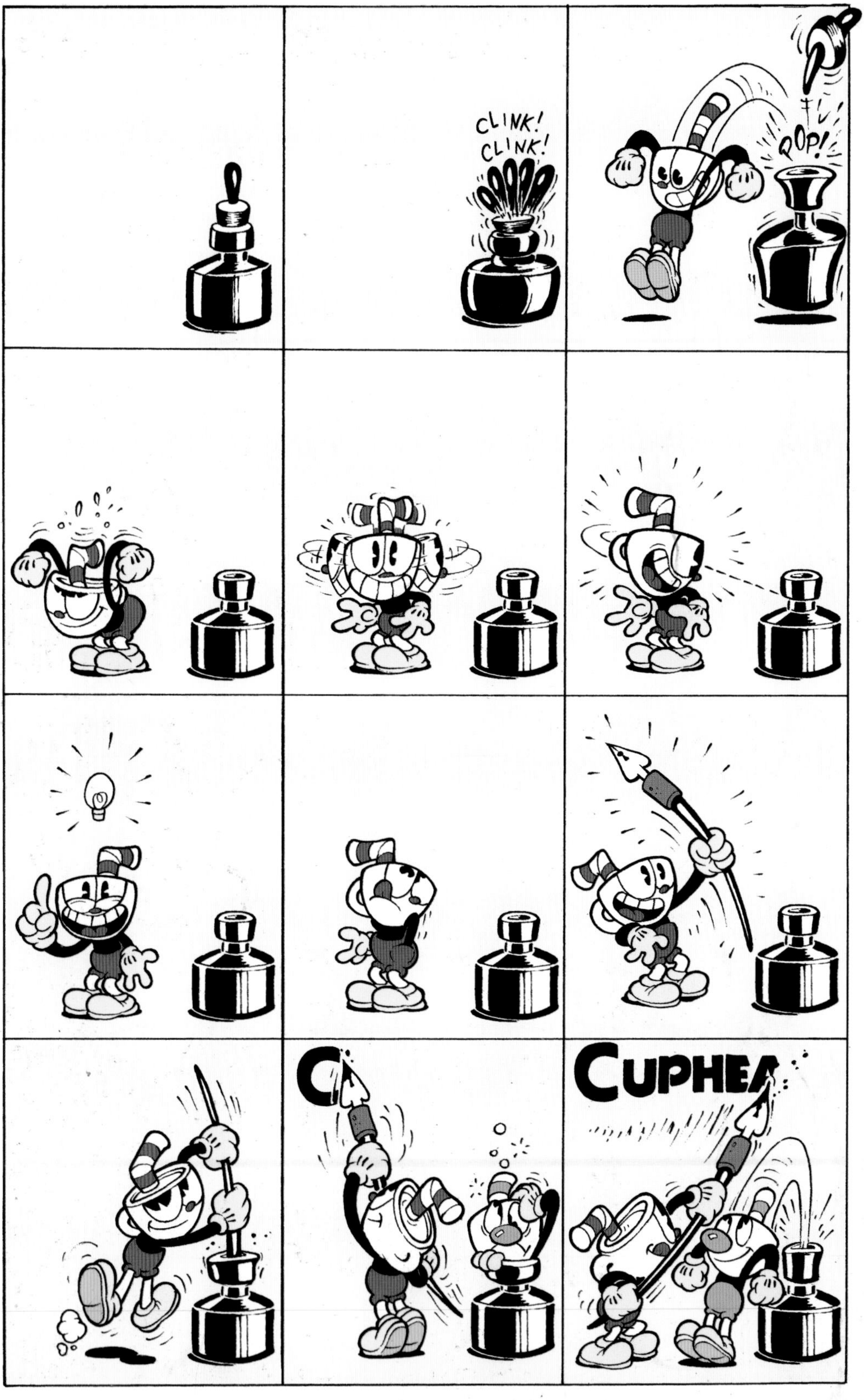
CLINK!
CLINK!
POP!
CUPHEA

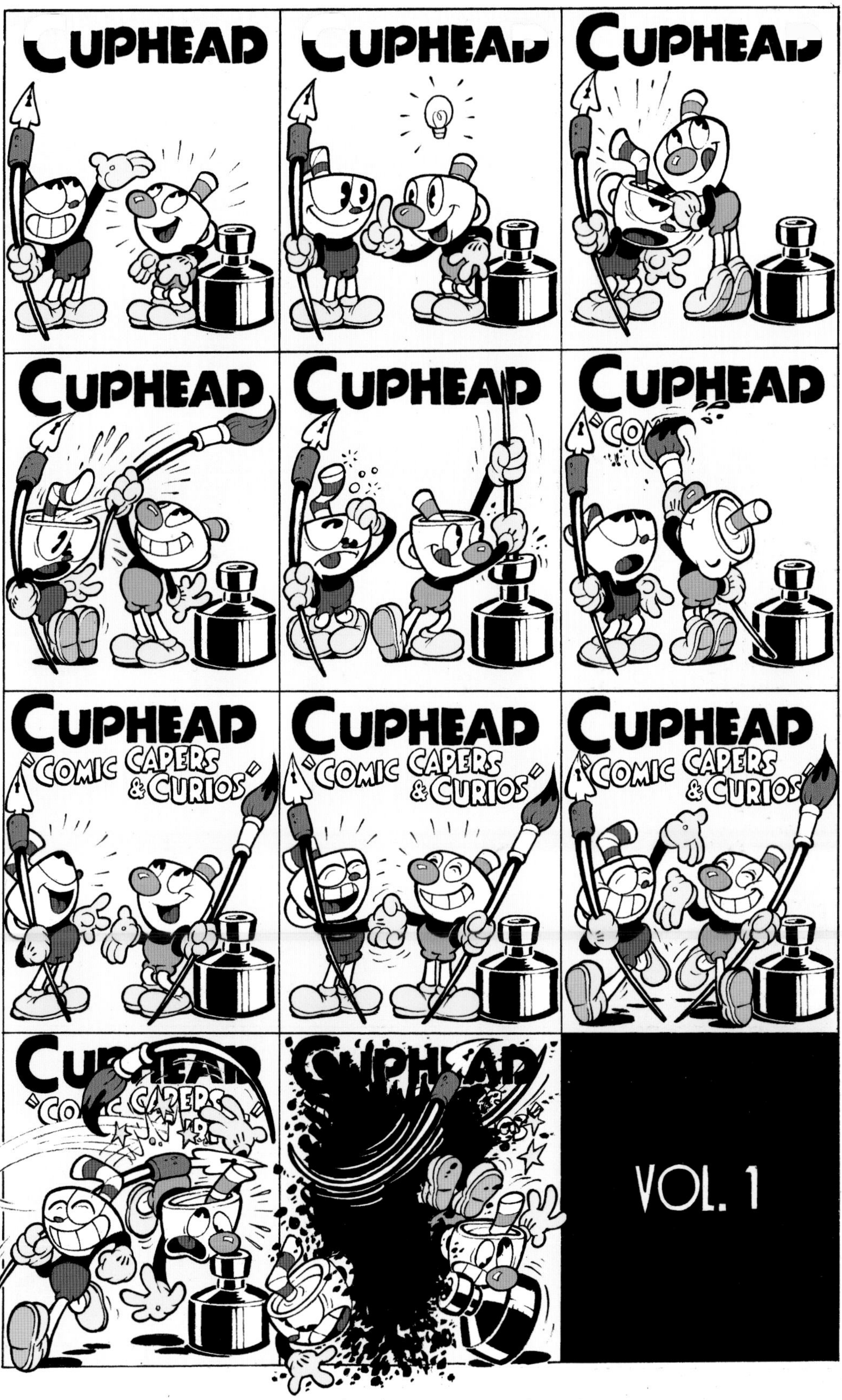
CUPHEAD
CUPHEAD
CUPHEAD
CUPHEAD
"COMIC CAPERS & CURIOS"
CUPHEAD
"COMIC CAPERS & CURIOS"
CUPHEAD
"COMIC CAPERS & CURIOS"
VOL. 1

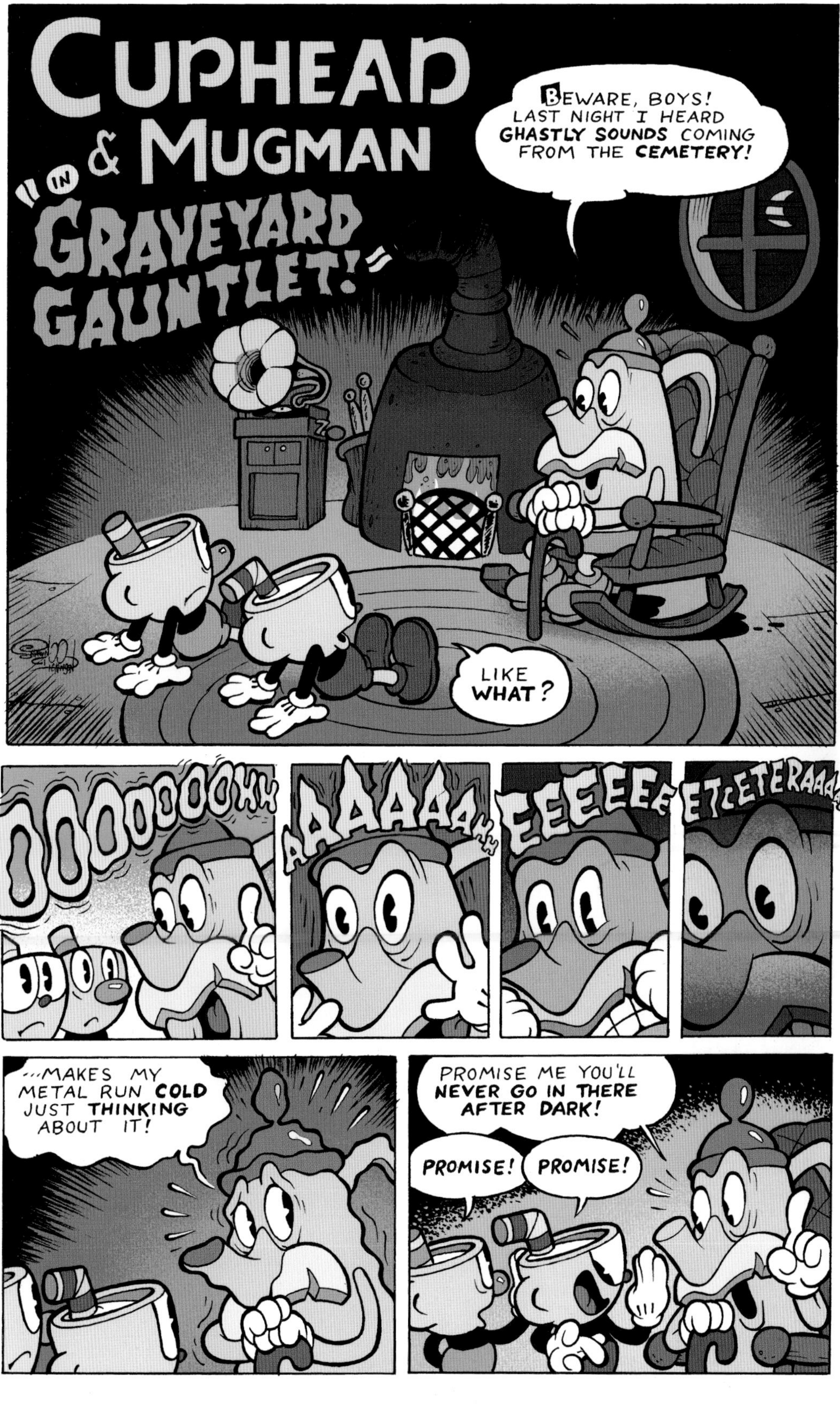

CUPHEAD
& MUGMAN
"IN
GRAVEYARD
GAUNTLET!"
BEWARE, BOYS! LAST NIGHT I HEARD GHASTLY SOUNDS COMING FROM THE CEMETERY!
LIKE WHAT?
OOOOOOOOHH
AAAAAAAHH
EEEEEEE
ETCETERAAAA!
...MAKES MY METAL RUN COLD JUST THINKING ABOUT IT!
PROMISE ME YOU'LL NEVER GO IN THERE AFTER DARK!
PROMISE!
PROMISE!

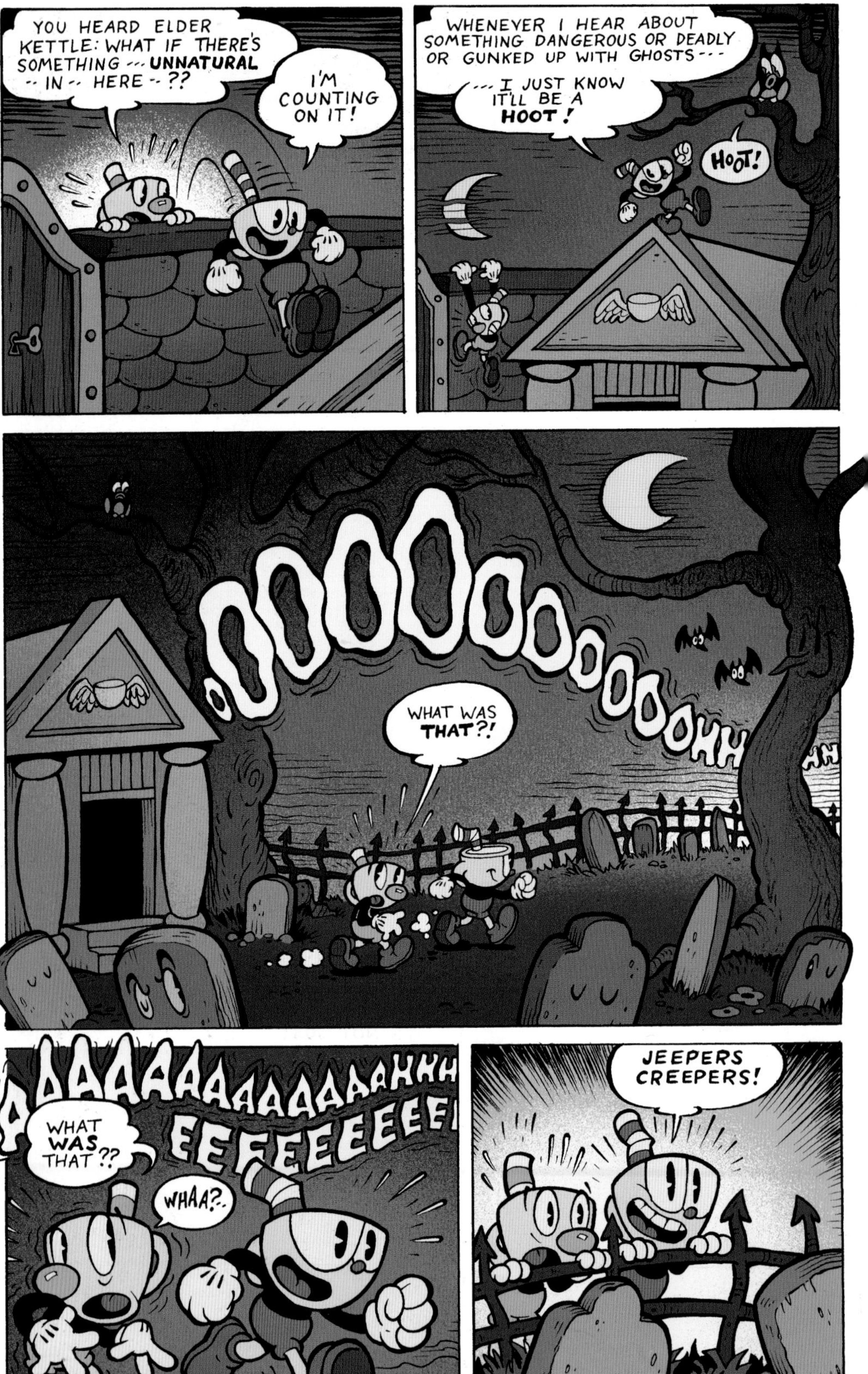
YOU HEARD ELDER KETTLE: WHAT IF THERE'S SOMETHING --- UNNATURAL -- IN -- HERE -- ??
I'M COUNTING ON IT!
WHENEVER I HEAR ABOUT SOMETHING DANGEROUS OR DEADLY OR GUNKED UP WITH GHOSTS---
--- I JUST KNOW IT'LL BE A HOOT!
HOOT!
OOOOOOOOOOOOOOHHHH
WHAT WAS THAT?!
AAAAAAAAAAAAAHHH
EEEEEEEEEE
WHAT WAS THAT??
WHAA?
JEEPERS CREEPERS!

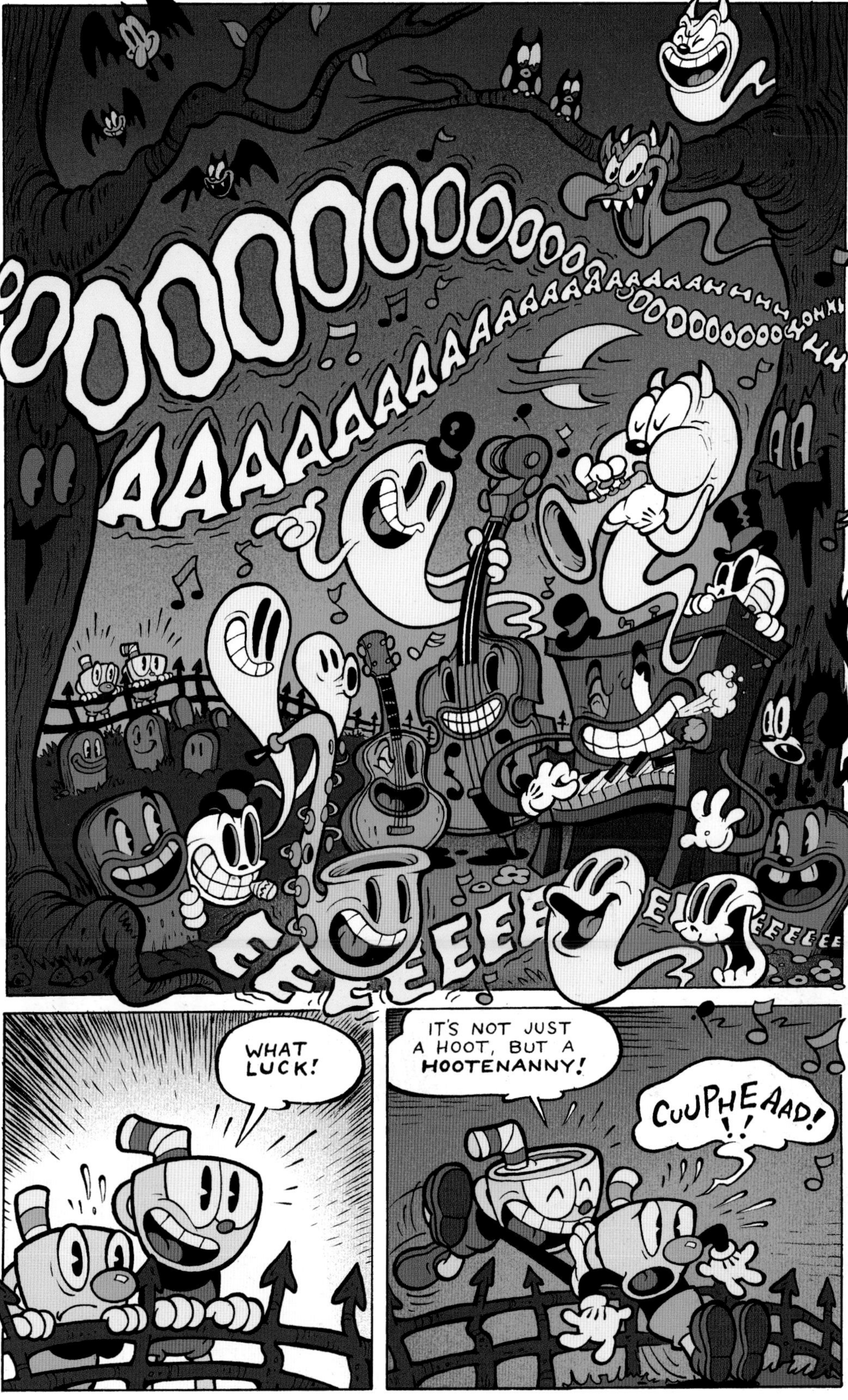
WHAT LUCK!
IT'S NOT JUST A HOOT, BUT A HOOTENANNY!
CUUPHEAAD!!!

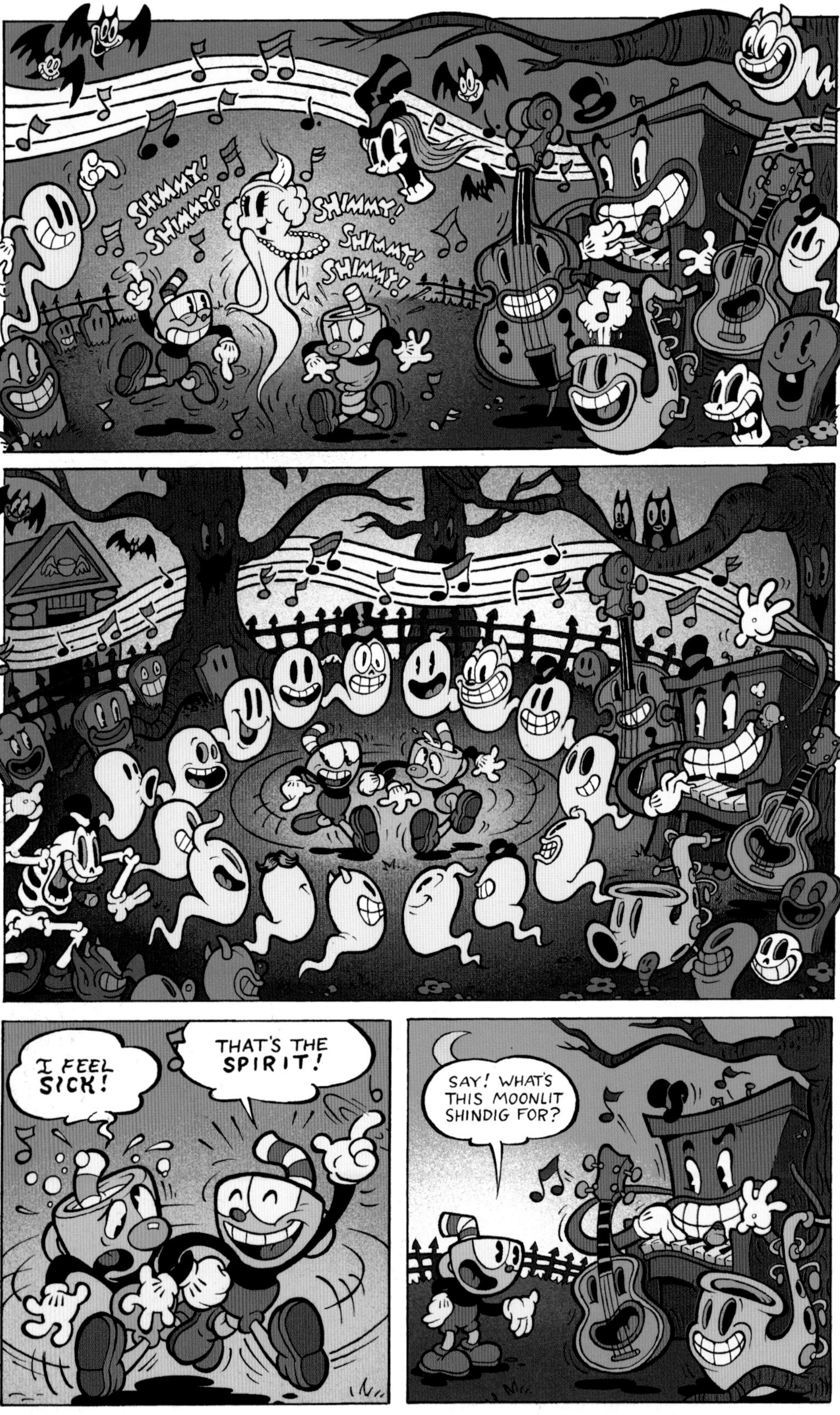

SHIMMY! SHIMMY!
SHIMMY! SHIMMY! SHIMMY!
I FEEL SICK!
THAT'S THE SPIRIT!
SAY! WHAT'S THIS MOONLIT SHINDIG FOR?

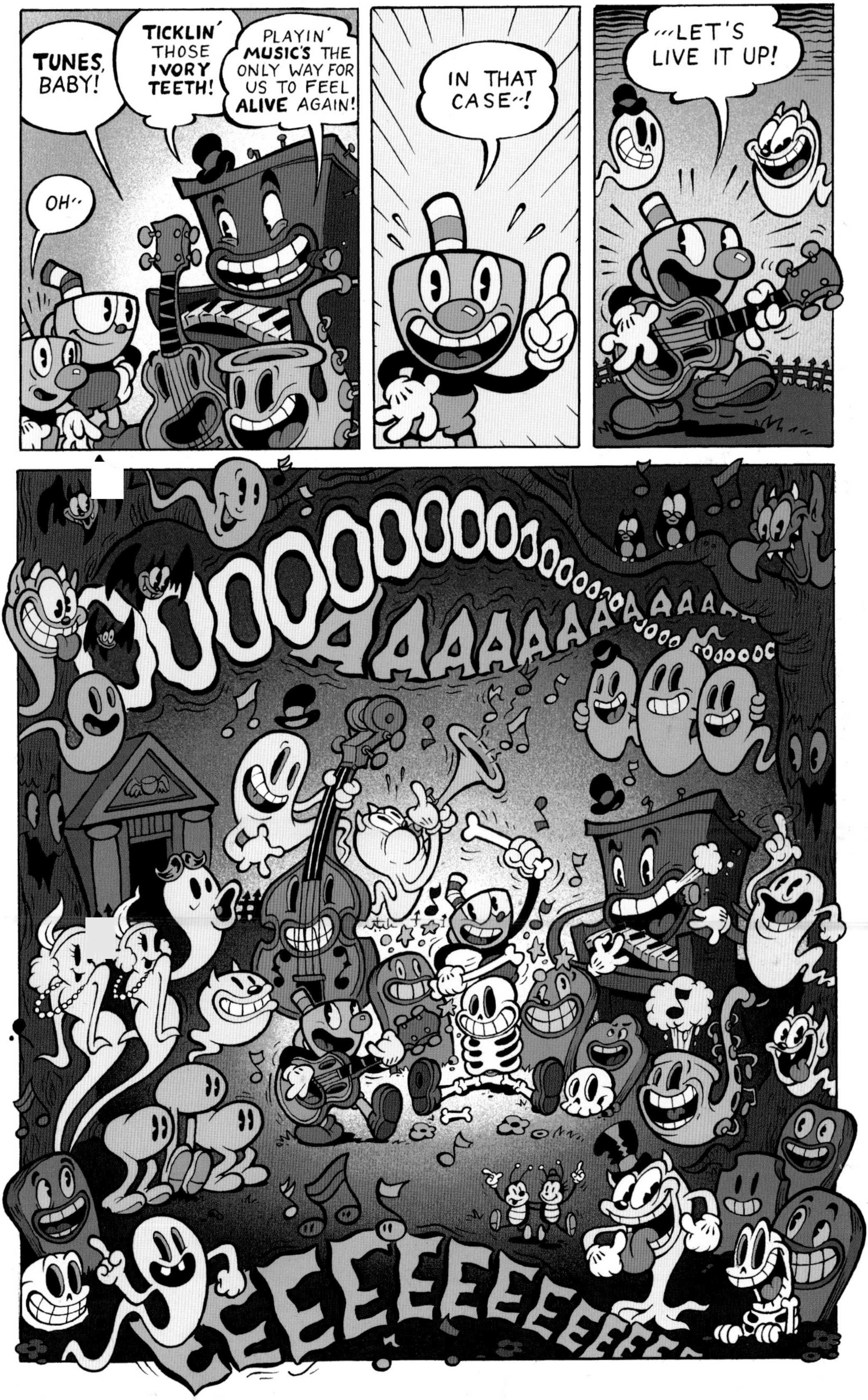

TUNES, BABY!
TICKLIN' THOSE IVORY TEETH!
PLAYIN' MUSIC'S THE ONLY WAY FOR US TO FEEL ALIVE AGAIN!
OH…
IN THAT CASE…!
…LET'S LIVE IT UP!
OOOOOOOOOOOOOOOOOOOO
AAAAAAAAAAAAAA
OOOOOOOOO
EEEEEEEEEEE

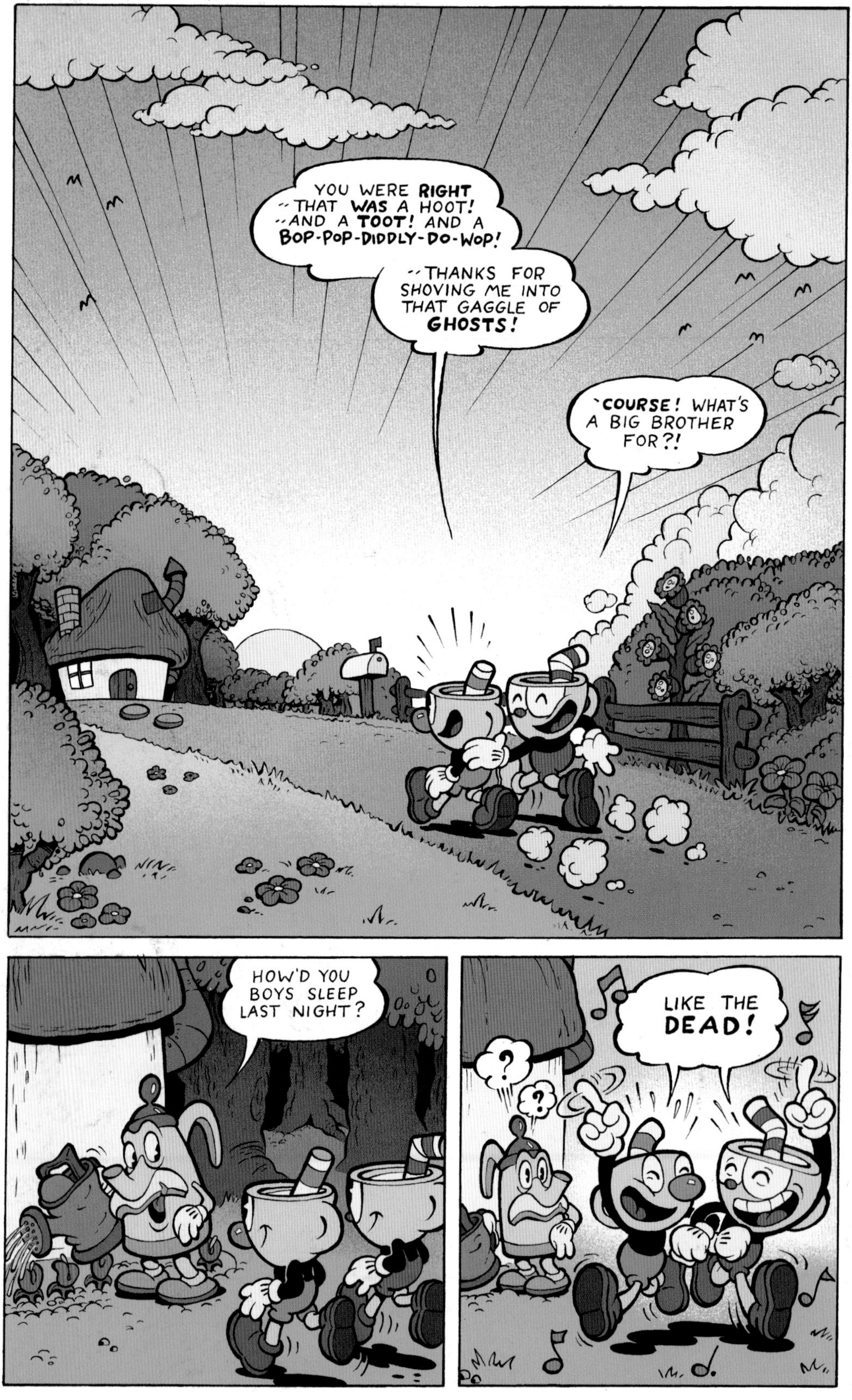
YOU WERE RIGHT --THAT WAS A HOOT! --AND A TOOT! AND A BOP-POP-DIDDLY-DO-WOP!
--THANKS FOR SHOVING ME INTO THAT GAGGLE OF GHOSTS!
`COURSE! WHAT'S A BIG BROTHER FOR?!
HOW'D YOU BOYS SLEEP LAST NIGHT?
LIKE THE DEAD!

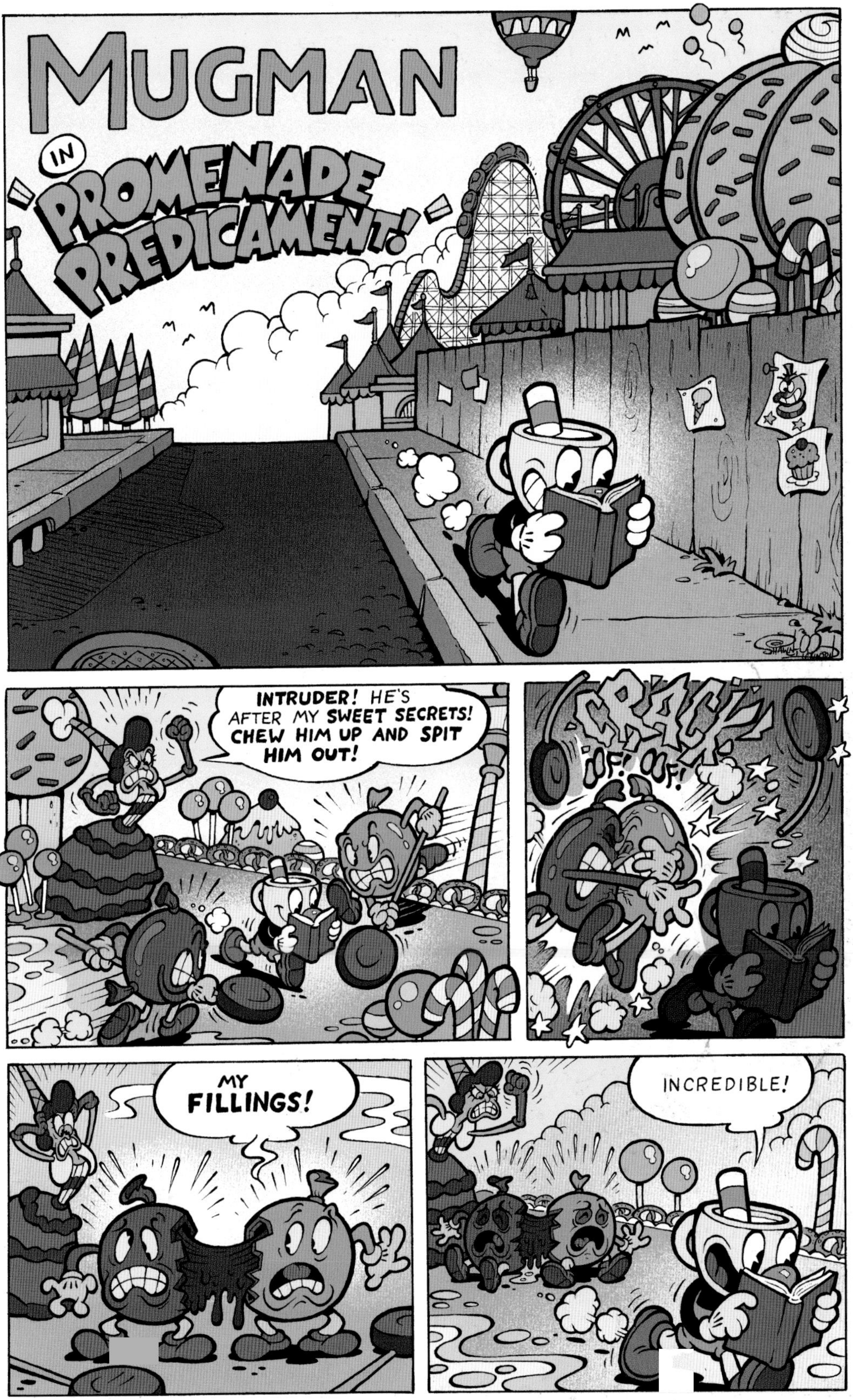
MUGMAN
IN
"PROMENADE PREDICAMENT!"
INTRUDER! HE'S AFTER MY SWEET SECRETS! CHEW HIM UP AND SPIT HIM OUT!
CRACK!
OOF! OOF!
MY FILLINGS!
INCREDIBLE!

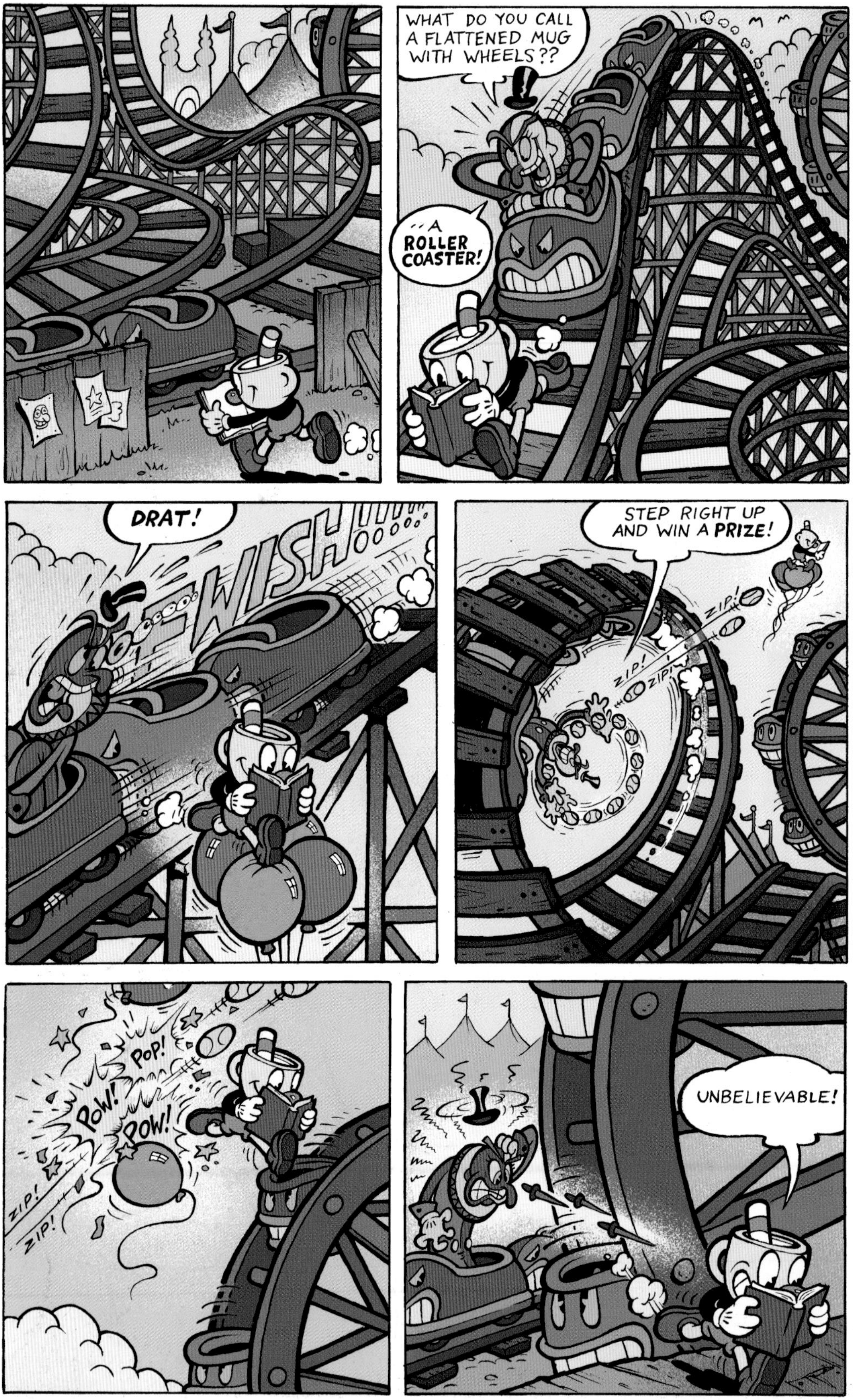
WHAT DO YOU CALL A FLATTENED MUG WITH WHEELS??
..A ROLLER COASTER!
DRAT!
FWISH!!!!!ooooooo
STEP RIGHT UP AND WIN A PRIZE!
ZIP!
ZIP!
ZIP!
POP!
POW!
POW!
ZIP!
ZIP!
UNBELIEVABLE!

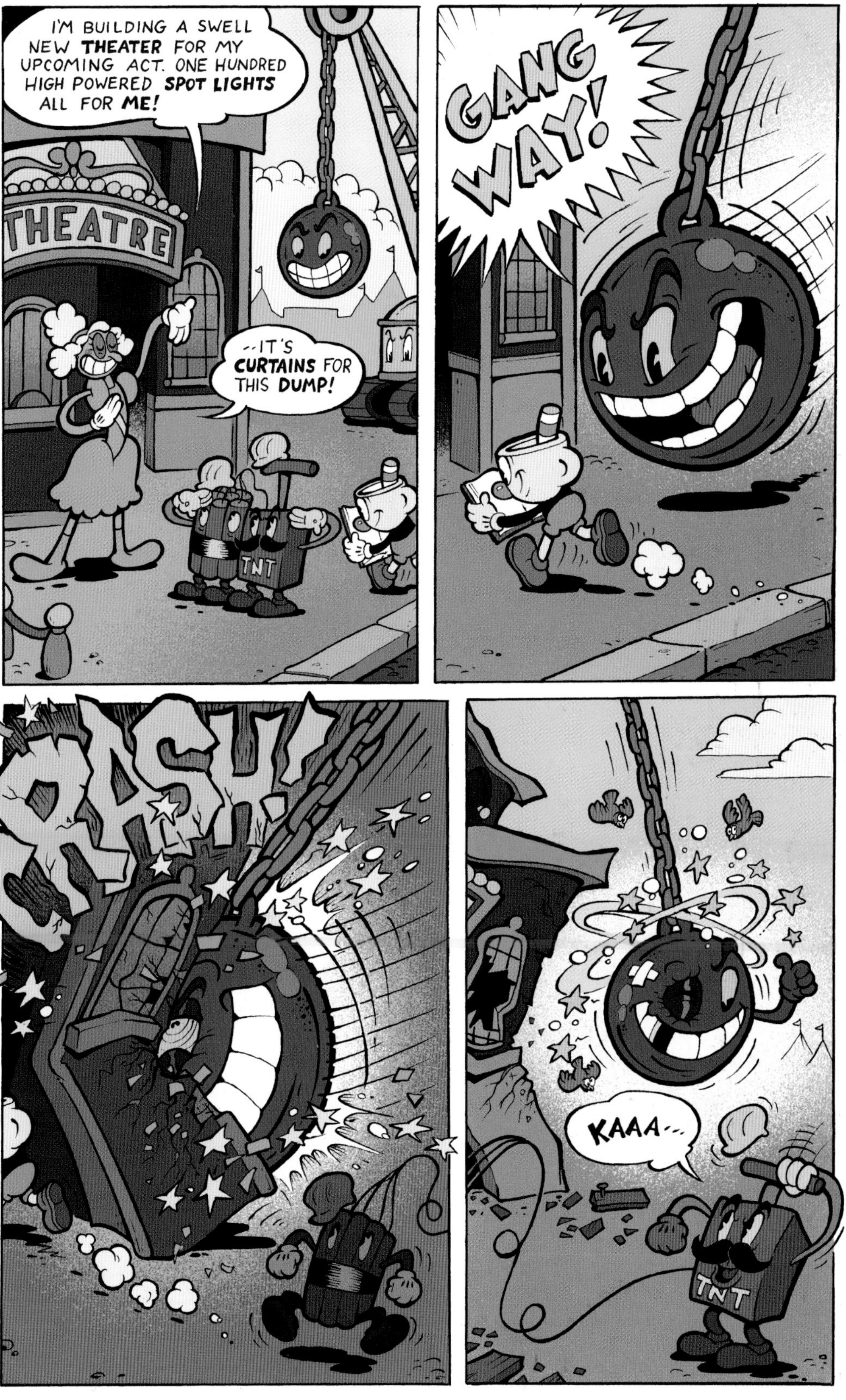
I'M BUILDING A SWELL NEW THEATER FOR MY UPCOMING ACT. ONE HUNDRED HIGH POWERED SPOT LIGHTS ALL FOR ME!
THEATRE
--IT'S CURTAINS FOR THIS DUMP!
TNT
GANG WAY!
KAAA--
TNT

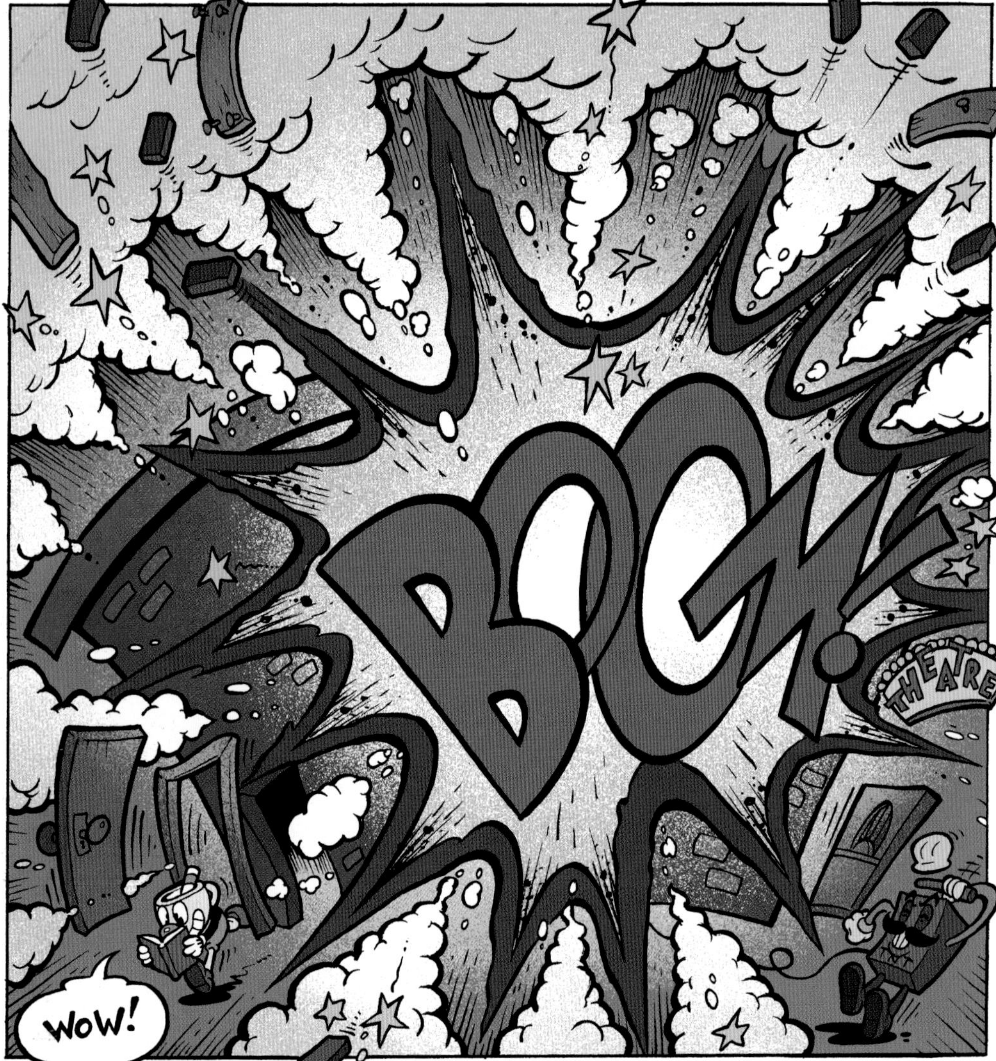
BOOM!
THEATRE
WOW!

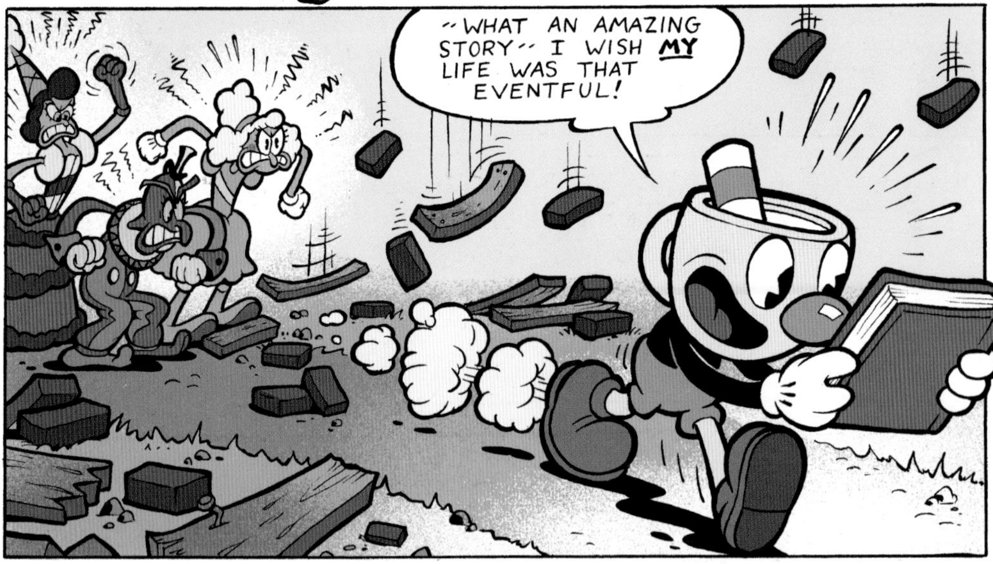
--WHAT AN AMAZING STORY-- I WISH **MY** LIFE WAS THAT EVENTFUL!

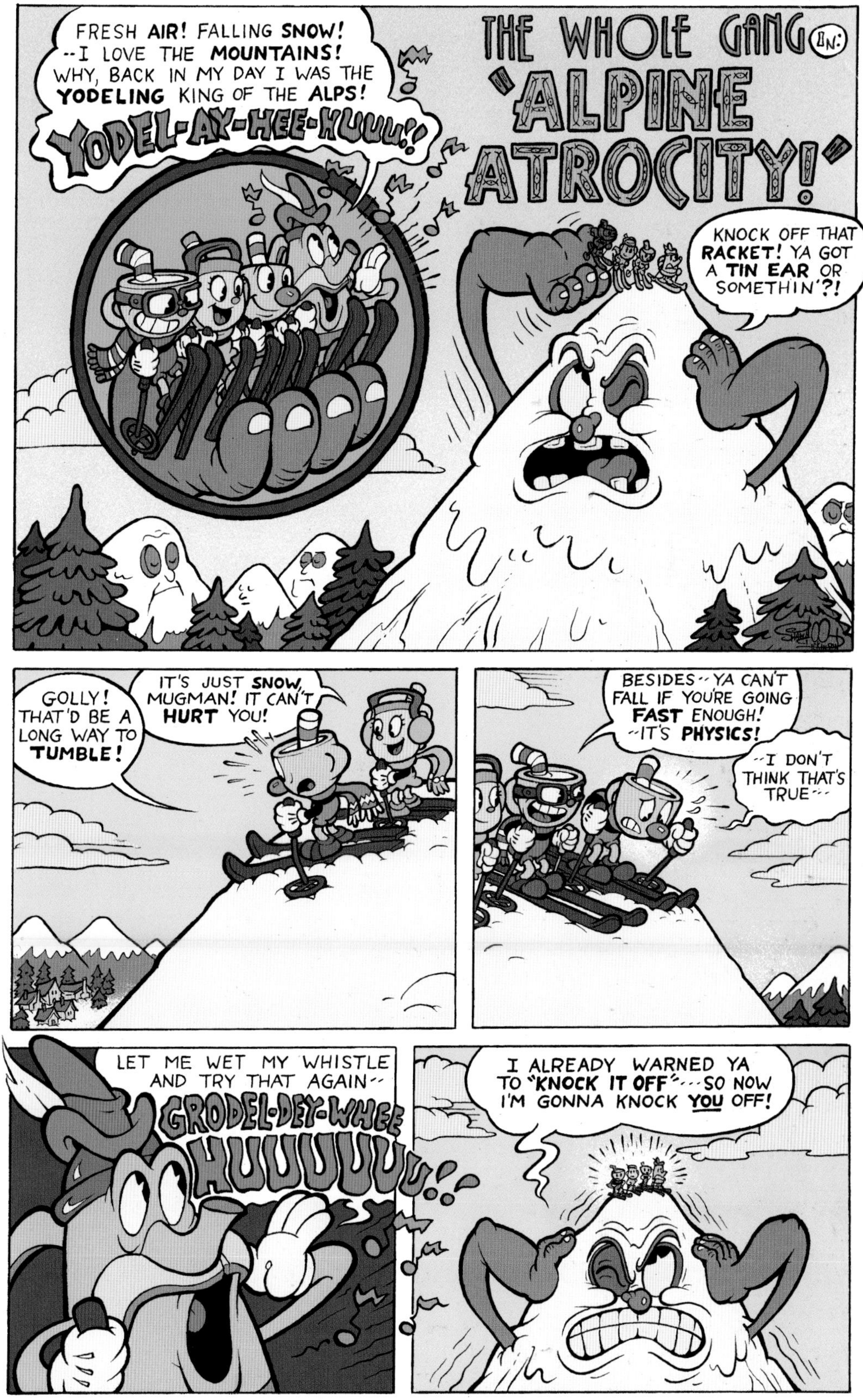

THE WHOLE GANG IN:
"ALPINE ATROCITY!"
FRESH AIR! FALLING SNOW! --I LOVE THE MOUNTAINS! WHY, BACK IN MY DAY I WAS THE YODELING KING OF THE ALPS!
YODEL-AY-HEE-HUUU!!
KNOCK OFF THAT RACKET! YA GOT A TIN EAR OR SOMETHIN'?!
GOLLY! THAT'D BE A LONG WAY TO TUMBLE!
IT'S JUST SNOW, MUGMAN! IT CAN'T HURT YOU!
BESIDES--YA CAN'T FALL IF YOU'RE GOING FAST ENOUGH! --IT'S PHYSICS!
--I DON'T THINK THAT'S TRUE--
LET ME WET MY WHISTLE AND TRY THAT AGAIN--
GRODEL-DEY-WHEE HUUUUUU!!
I ALREADY WARNED YA TO "KNOCK IT OFF"---SO NOW I'M GONNA KNOCK YOU OFF!

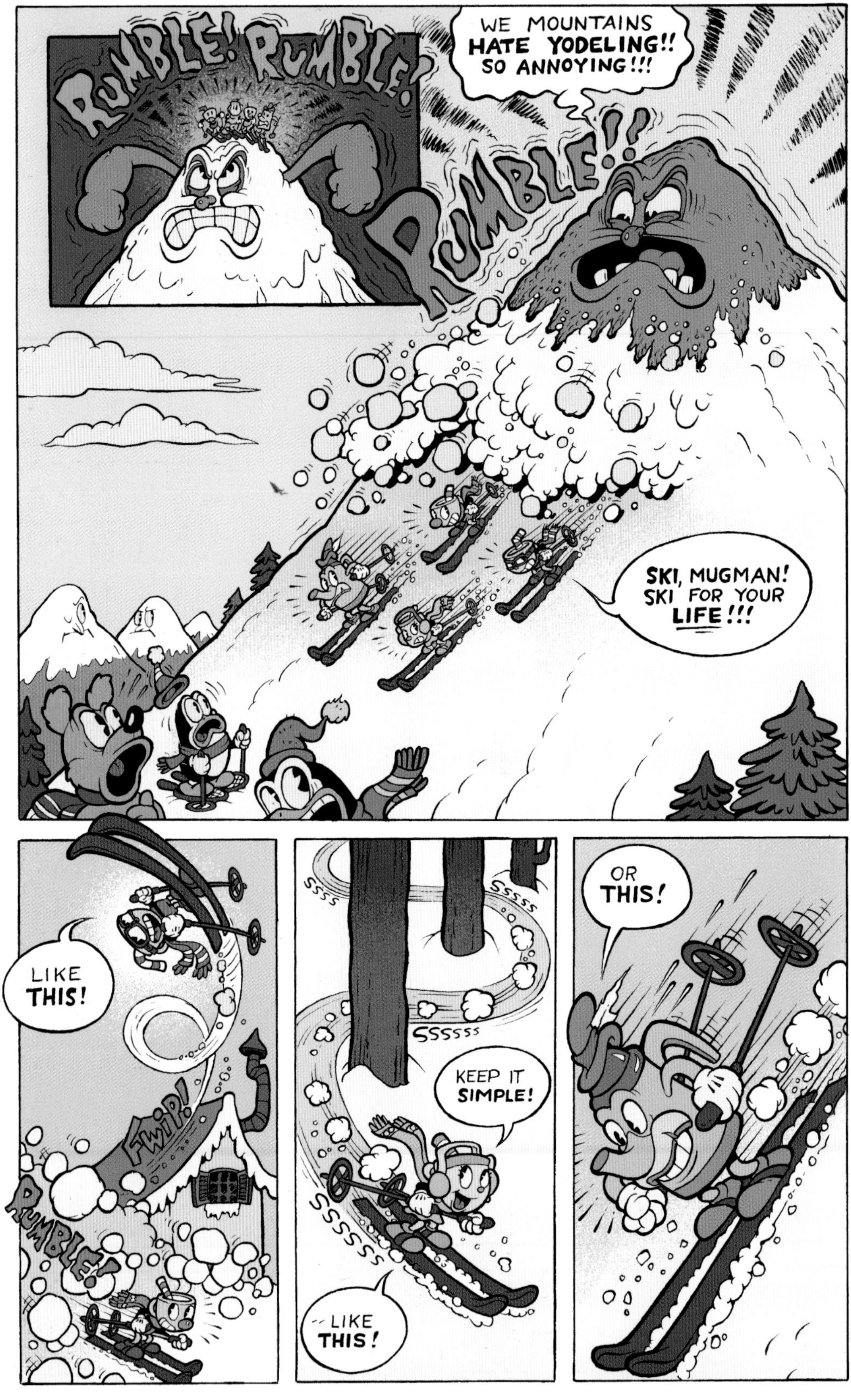

RUMBLE! RUMBLE!
WE MOUNTAINS HATE YODELING!! SO ANNOYING!!!
RUMBLE!!
SKI, MUGMAN! SKI FOR YOUR LIFE!!!
LIKE THIS!
FWIP!
RUMBLE!
SSSS
SSSSS
SSSSSS
KEEP IT SIMPLE!
SSSSSS
LIKE THIS!
OR THIS!

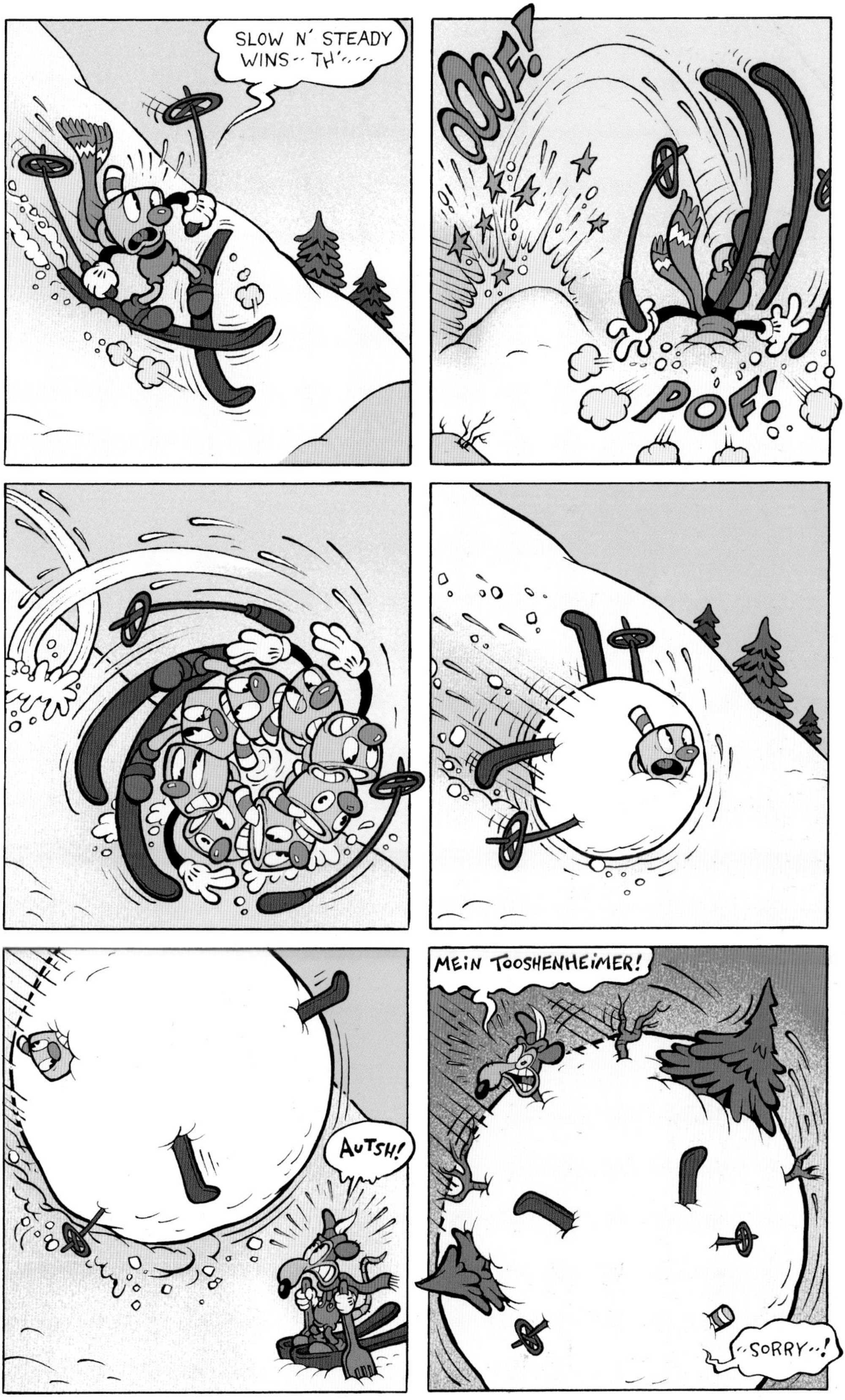
SLOW N' STEADY WINS-- TH'-----
OOOF!
POF!
AUTSH!
MEIN TOOSHENHEIMER!
--SORRY--!

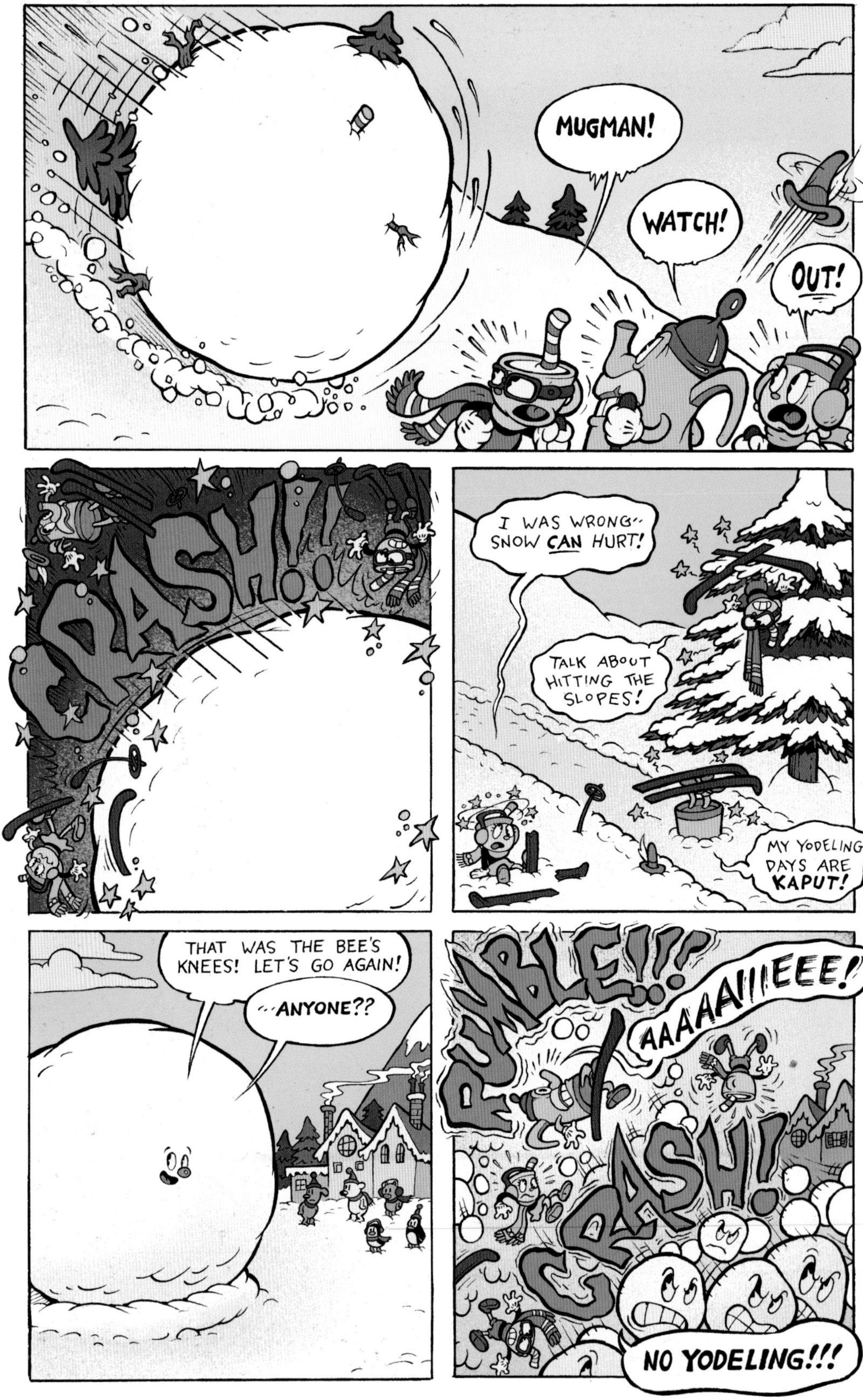
MUGMAN!
WATCH!
OUT!
CRASH!!!
I WAS WRONG... SNOW CAN HURT!
TALK ABOUT HITTING THE SLOPES!
MY YODELING DAYS ARE KAPUT!
THAT WAS THE BEE'S KNEES! LET'S GO AGAIN!
...ANYONE??
RUMBLE!!!
AAAAA!!!EEE!
CRASH!
NO YODELING!!!

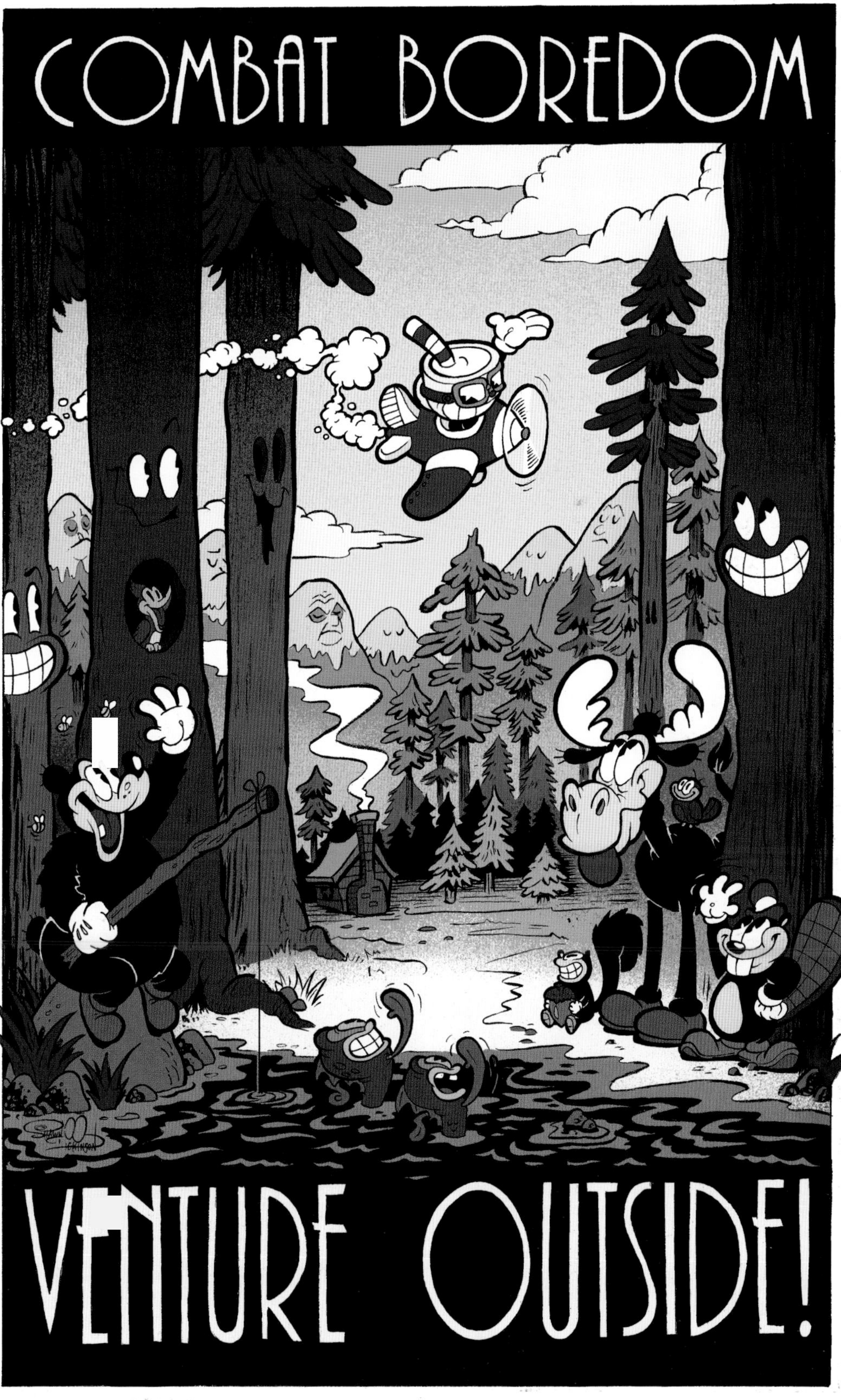
COMBAT BOREDOM
VENTURE OUTSIDE!

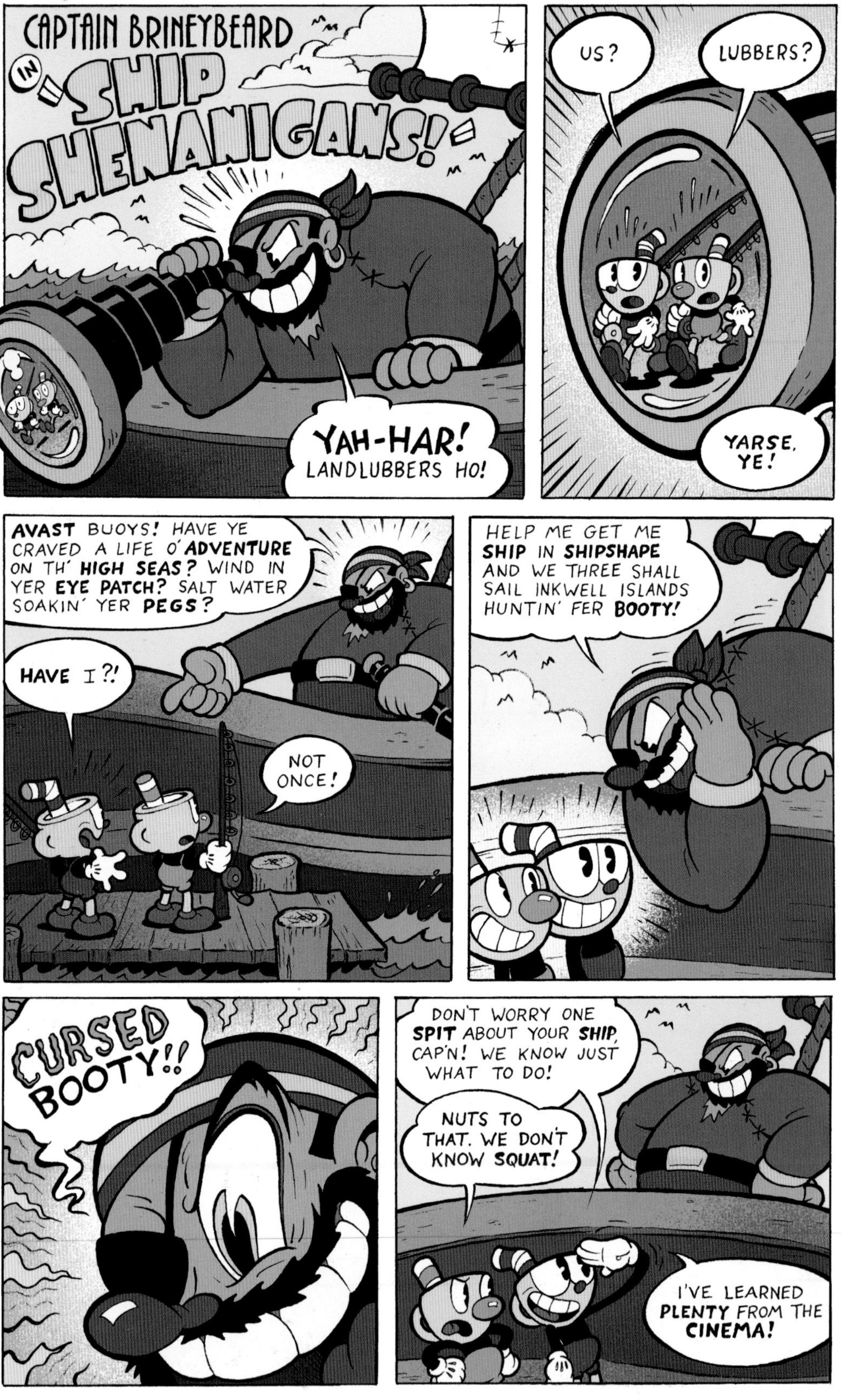
CAPTAIN BRINEYBEARD
IN "SHIP SHENANIGANS!"
YAH-HAR! LANDLUBBERS HO!
US?
LUBBERS?
YARSE, YE!
AVAST BUOYS! HAVE YE CRAVED A LIFE O' ADVENTURE ON TH' HIGH SEAS? WIND IN YER EYE PATCH? SALT WATER SOAKIN' YER PEGS?
HAVE I?!
NOT ONCE!
HELP ME GET ME SHIP IN SHIPSHAPE AND WE THREE SHALL SAIL INKWELL ISLANDS HUNTIN' FER BOOTY!
CURSED BOOTY!!
DON'T WORRY ONE SPIT ABOUT YOUR SHIP, CAP'N! WE KNOW JUST WHAT TO DO!
NUTS TO THAT. WE DON'T KNOW SQUAT!
I'VE LEARNED PLENTY FROM THE CINEMA!

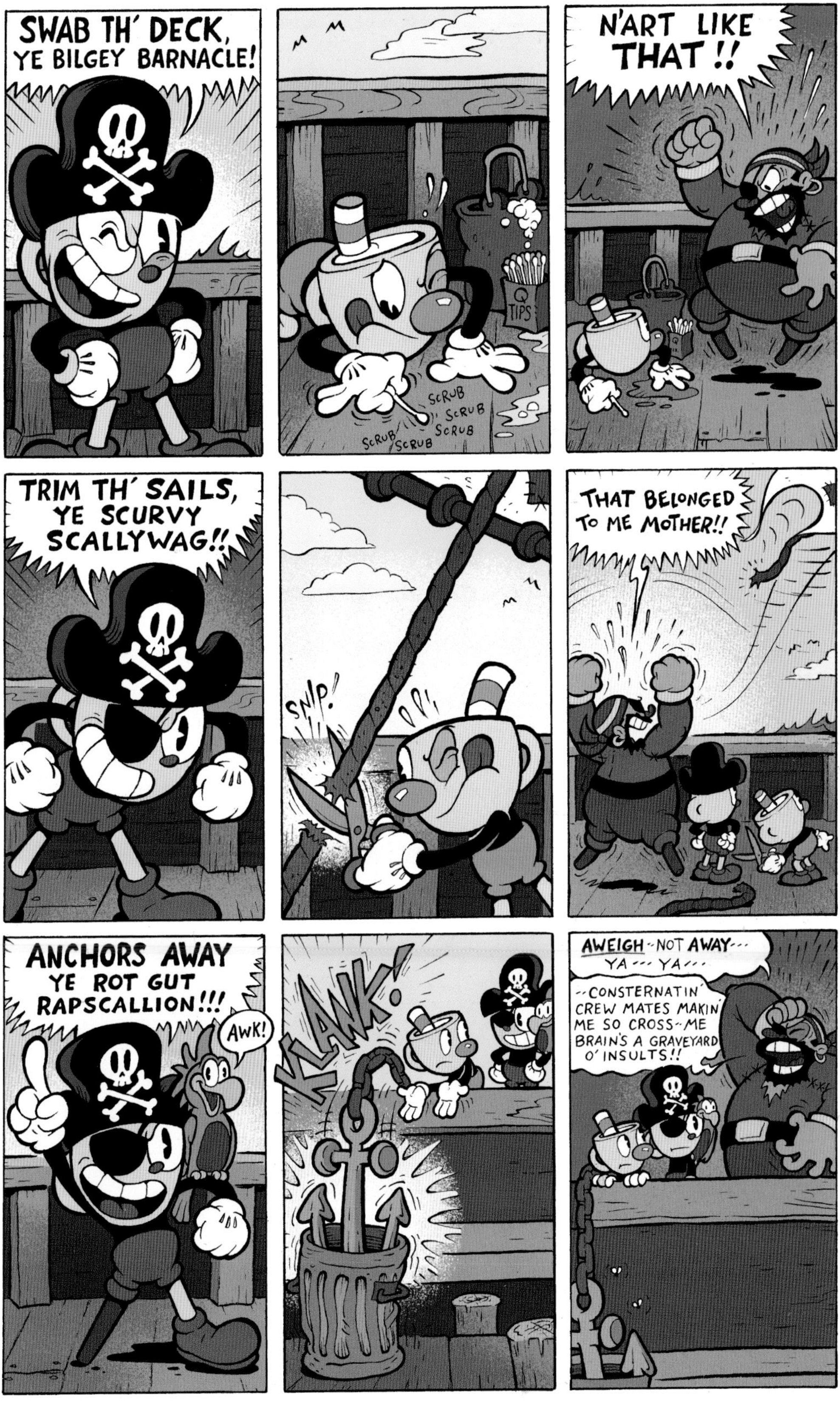
SWAB TH' DECK, YE BILGEY BARNACLE!
SCRUB SCRUB SCRUB SCRUB SCRUB SCRUB
Q TIPS
N'ART LIKE THAT!!
TRIM TH' SAILS, YE SCURVY SCALLYWAG!!
SNIP!
THAT BELONGED TO ME MOTHER!!
ANCHORS AWAY YE ROT GUT RAPSCALLION!!!
AWK!
KLANK!
AWEIGH -- NOT AWAY --- YA --- YA ---
-- CONSTERNATIN' CREW MATES MAKIN ME SO CROSS -- ME BRAIN'S A GRAVEYARD O' INSULTS!!

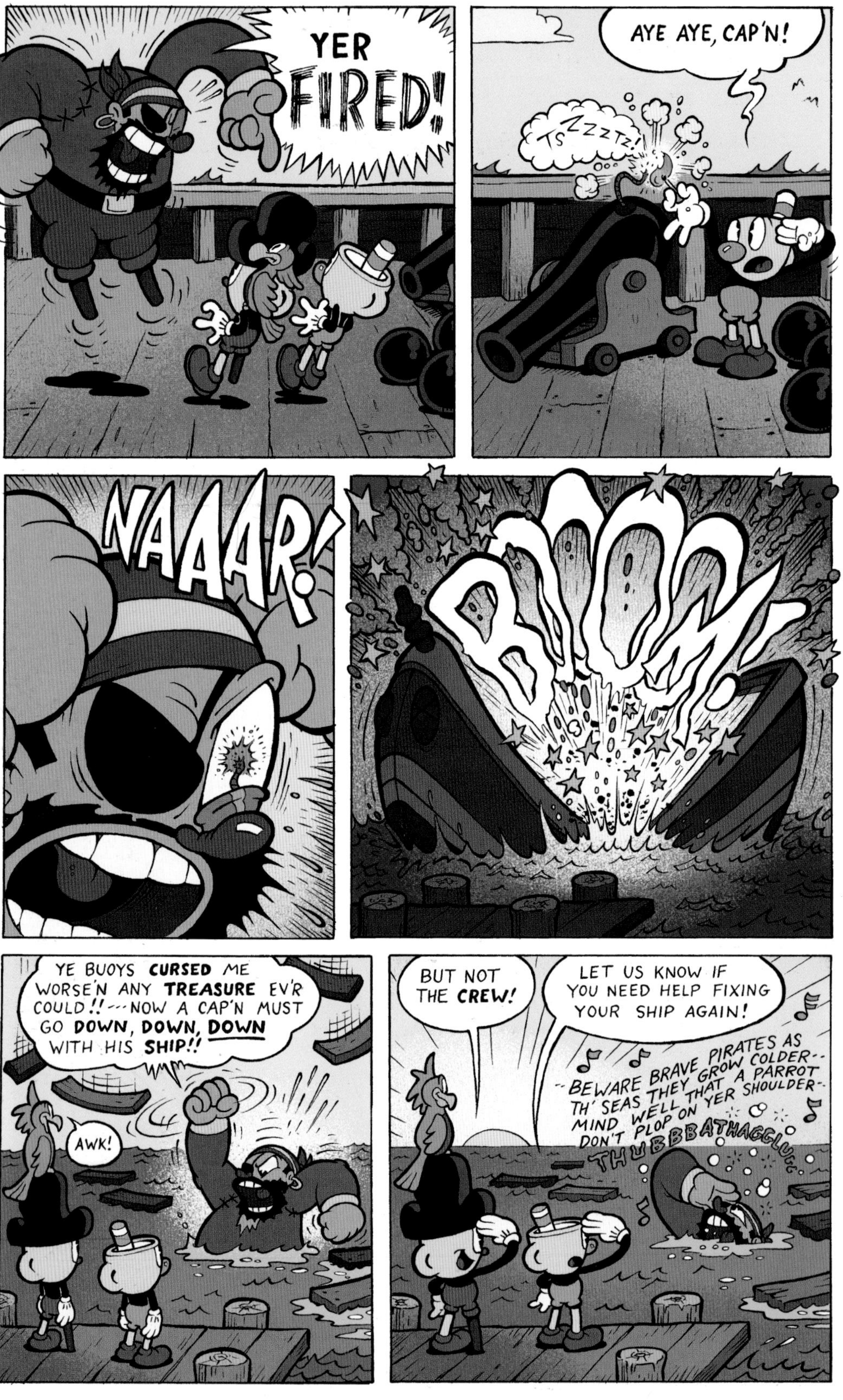

YER FIRED!
AYE AYE, CAP'N!
TSZZZZTZ!
NAAAR!
BOOOM!
YE BUOYS CURSED ME WORSE'N ANY TREASURE EV'R COULD!!--- NOW A CAP'N MUST GO DOWN, DOWN, DOWN WITH HIS SHIP!!
AWK!
BUT NOT THE CREW!
LET US KNOW IF YOU NEED HELP FIXING YOUR SHIP AGAIN!
-BEWARE BRAVE PIRATES AS TH' SEAS THEY GROW COLDER--
MIND WELL THAT A PARROT DON'T PLOP ON YER SHOULDER-
THUBBBATHAGGLUG

CUPHEAD
IN
"SCRAPYARD SCRAP!"
LET'S SEE WHAT THIS BABY'S GOT!
LOOP-DE-LOO!
CORKSCREW!
BOOM!
BZZZ
ZZZT
CRASH LANDING??
PFOOM!

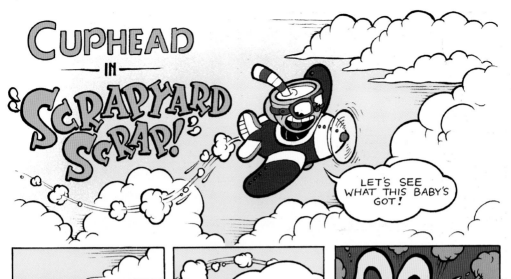

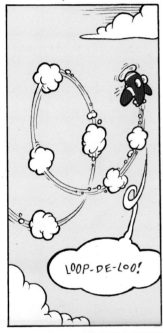

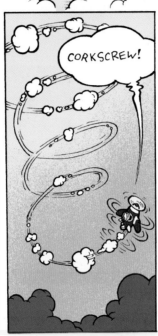

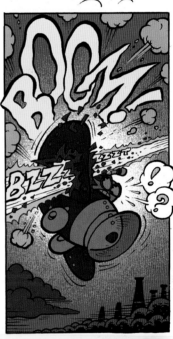

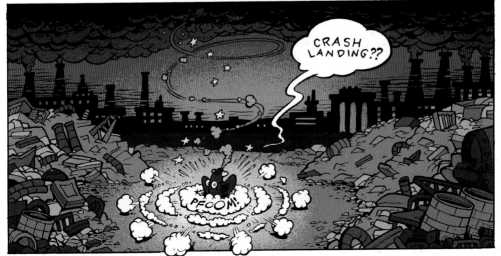

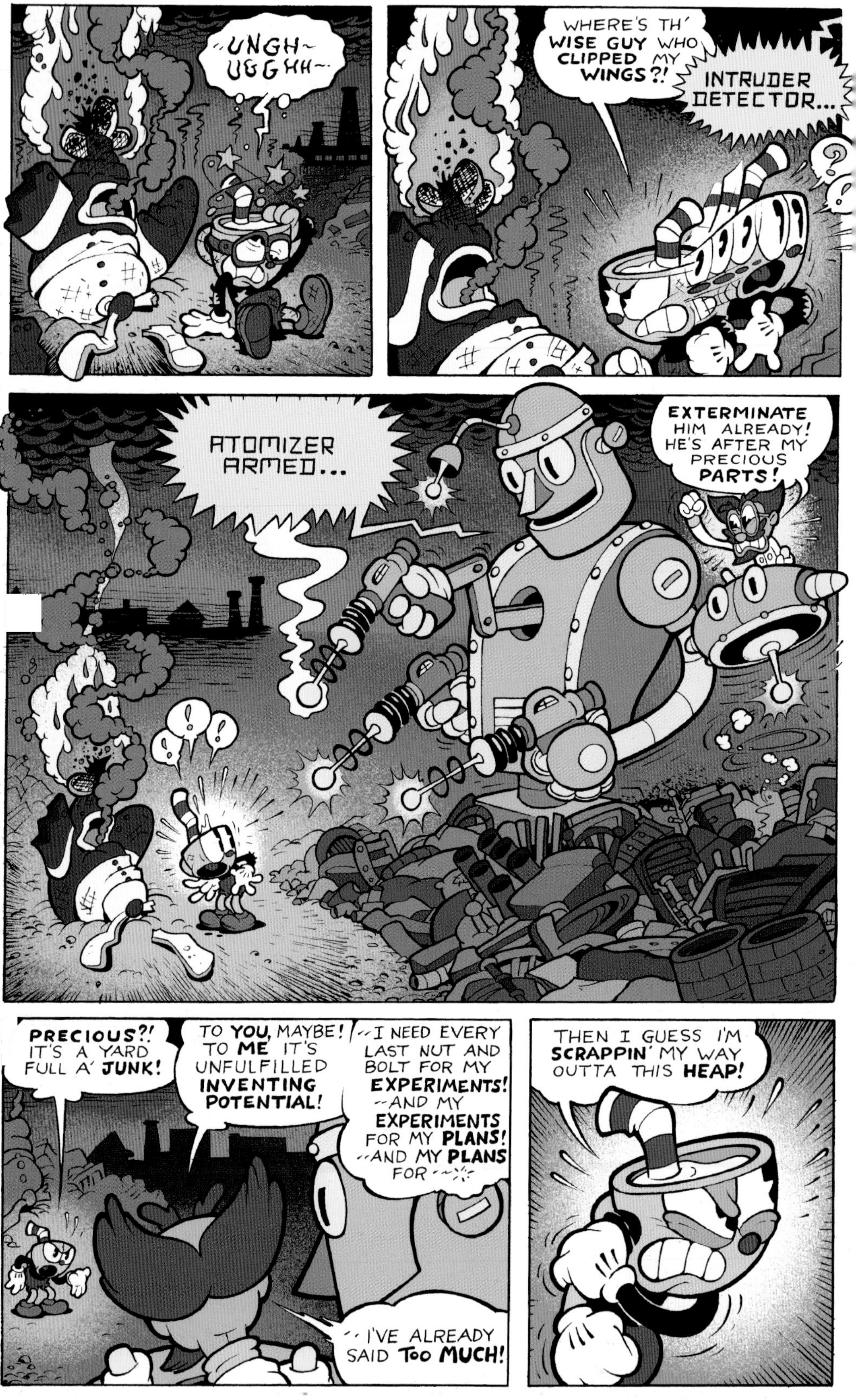
UNGH~ UGGHH~
WHERE'S TH' WISE GUY WHO CLIPPED MY WINGS?!
INTRUDER DETECTOR...
ATOMIZER ARMED...
EXTERMINATE HIM ALREADY! HE'S AFTER MY PRECIOUS PARTS!
PRECIOUS?! IT'S A YARD FULL A' JUNK!
TO YOU, MAYBE! TO ME IT'S UNFULFILLED INVENTING POTENTIAL!
--I NEED EVERY LAST NUT AND BOLT FOR MY EXPERIMENTS! --AND MY EXPERIMENTS FOR MY PLANS! --AND MY PLANS FOR--
--I'VE ALREADY SAID TOO MUCH!
THEN I GUESS I'M SCRAPPIN' MY WAY OUTTA THIS HEAP!

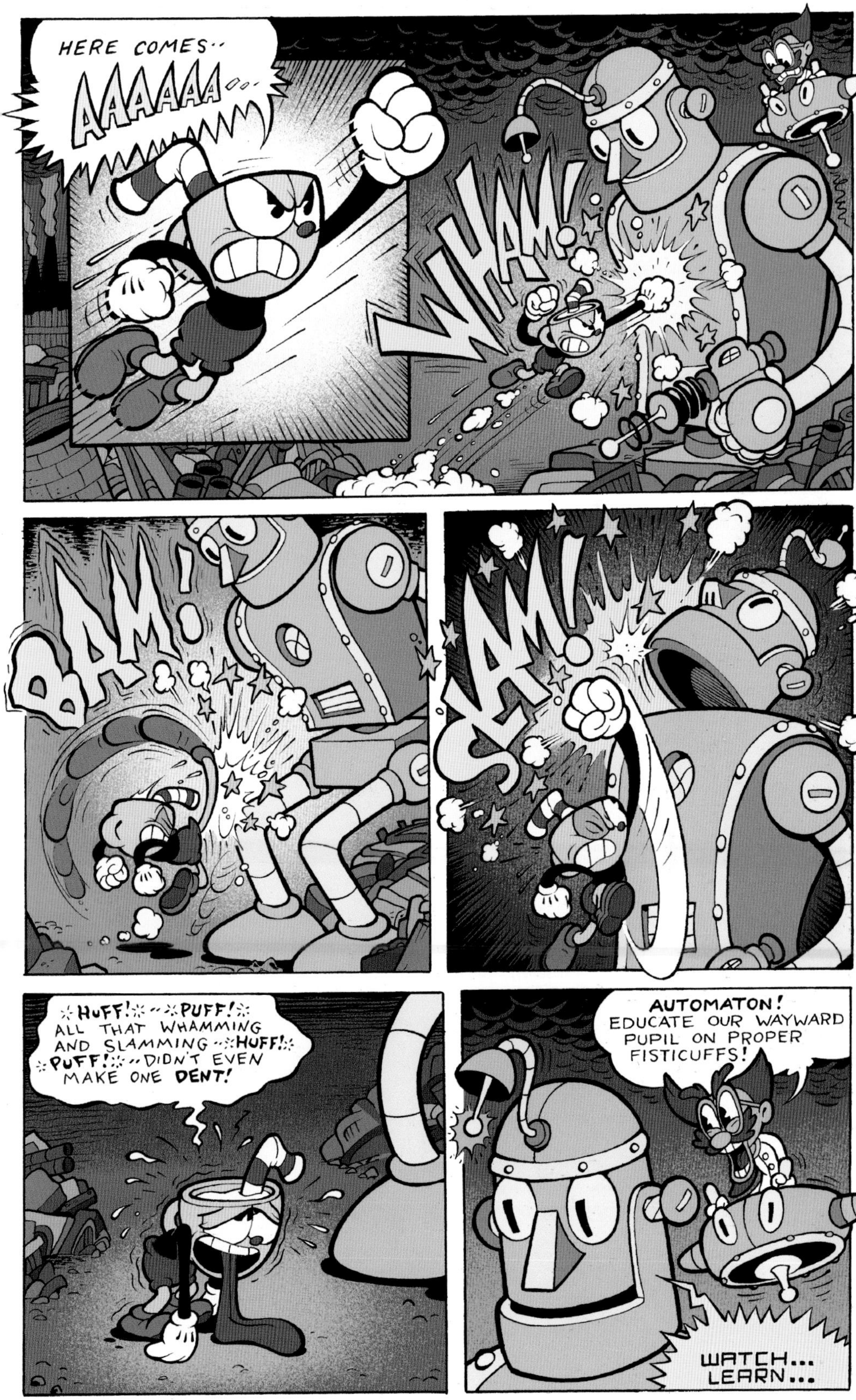
HERE COMES..
AAAAAA
WHAM!
BAM!
SLAM!
HUFF! -- PUFF!
ALL THAT WHAMMING AND SLAMMING -- HUFF! PUFF! -- DIDN'T EVEN MAKE ONE DENT!
AUTOMATON! EDUCATE OUR WAYWARD PUPIL ON PROPER FISTICUFFS!
WATCH... LEARN...

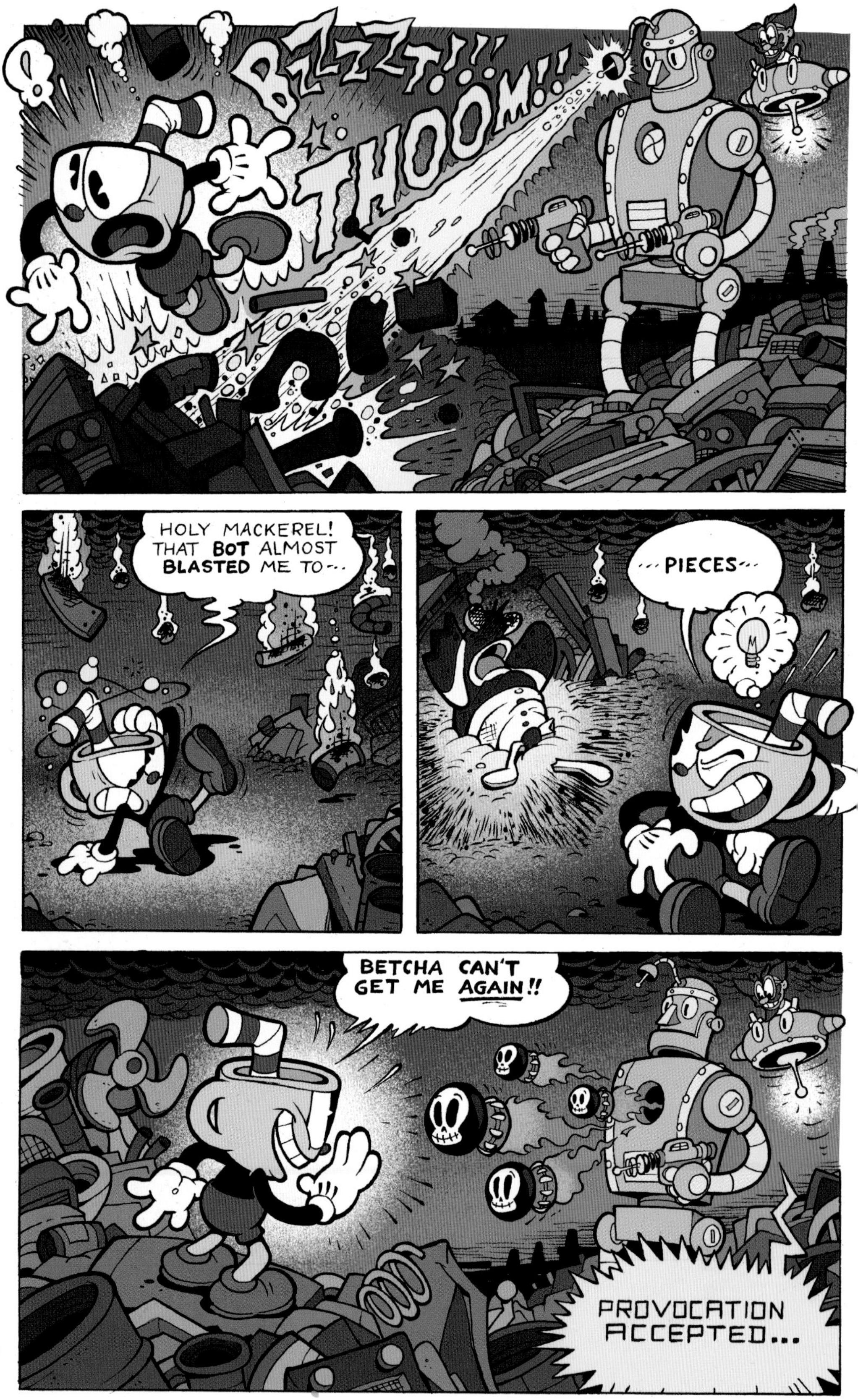
BZZZZT!!!
THOOOM!!
HOLY MACKEREL! THAT BOT ALMOST BLASTED ME TO--
--PIECES--
BETCHA CAN'T GET ME AGAIN!!
PROVOCATION ACCEPTED...

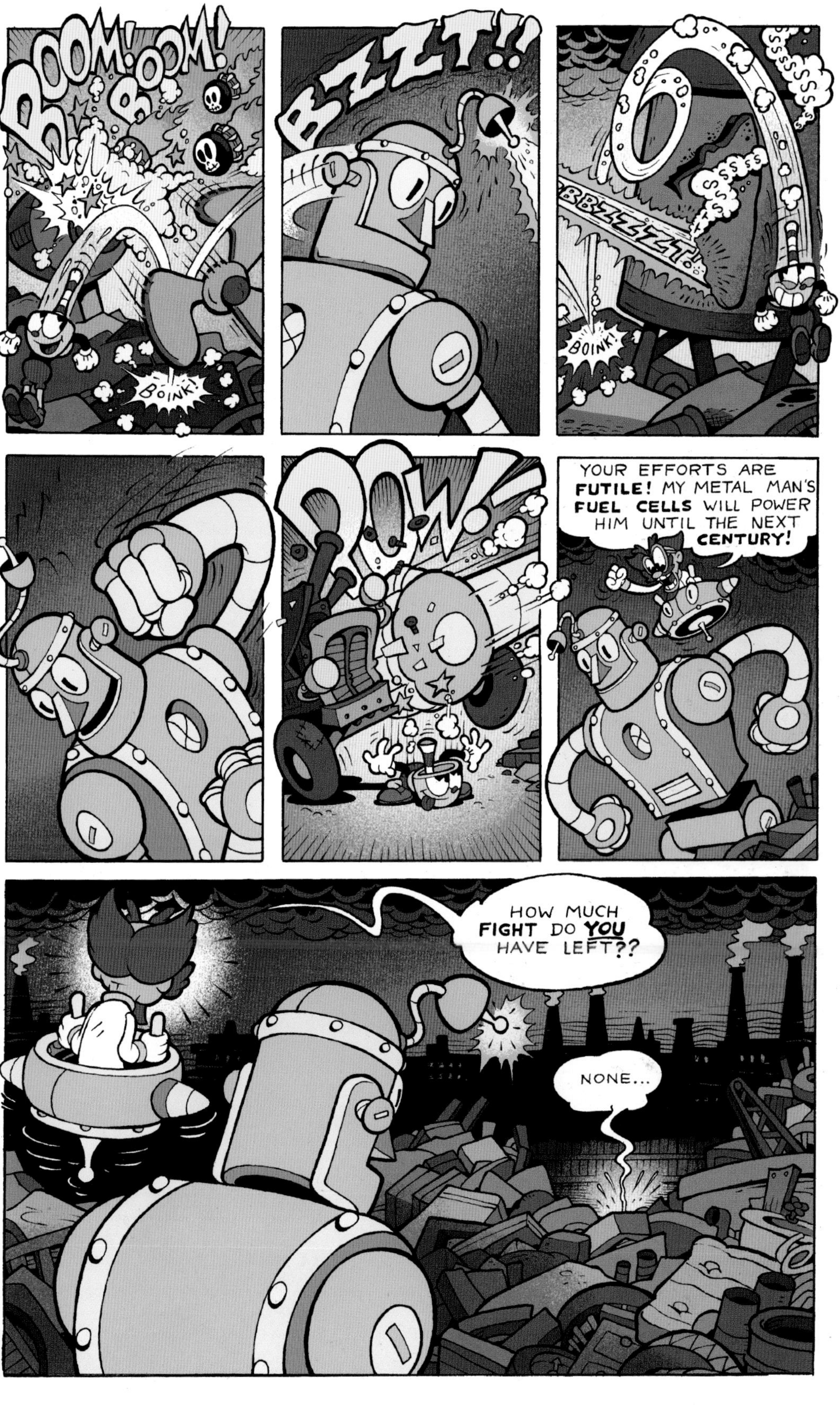
BOOM! BOOM!
BOINK!
BZZZT!!
SSSSSSSS
BOINK!
POW!
YOUR EFFORTS ARE FUTILE! MY METAL MAN'S FUEL CELLS WILL POWER HIM UNTIL THE NEXT CENTURY!
HOW MUCH FIGHT DO YOU HAVE LEFT??
NONE...

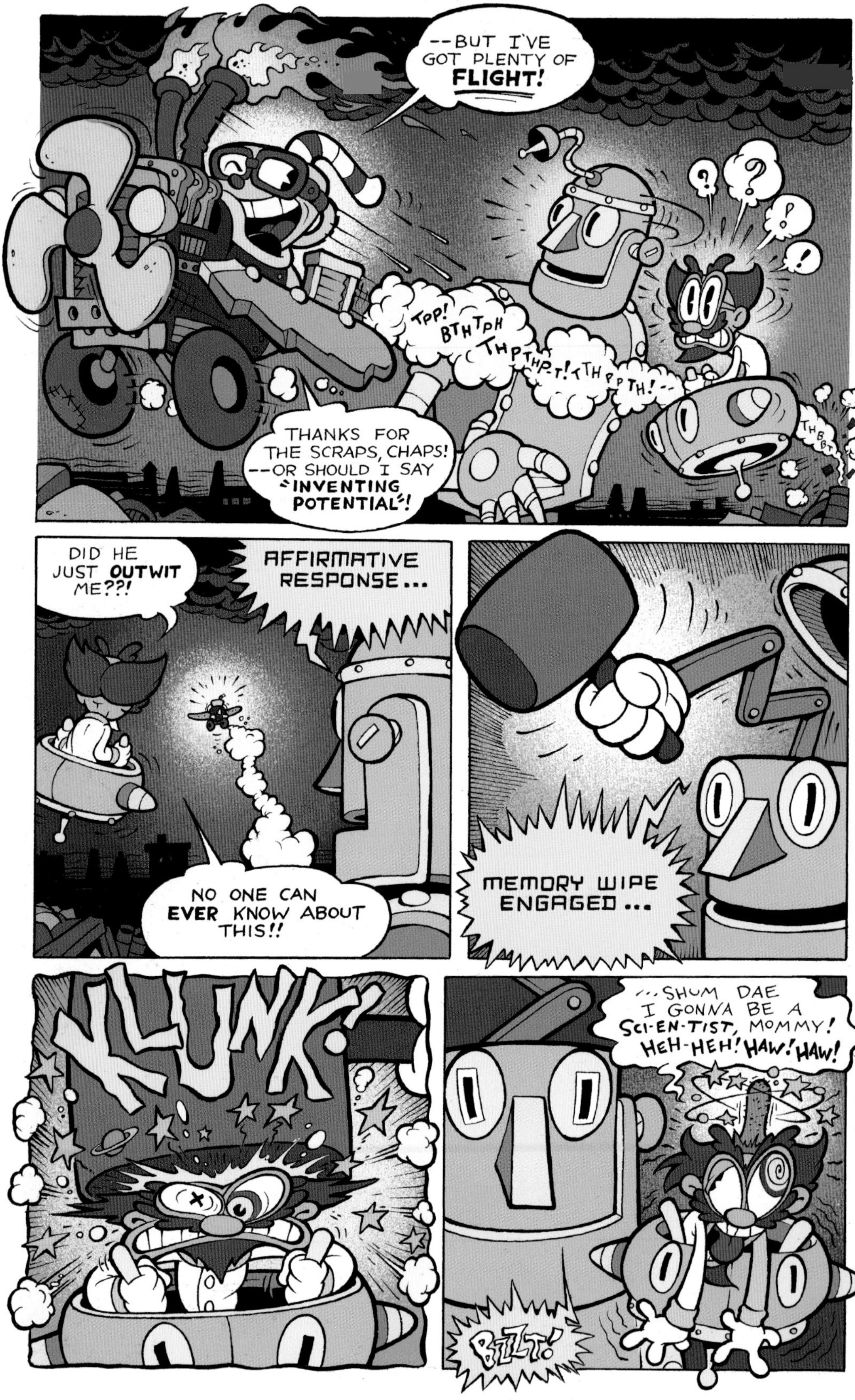

--BUT I'VE GOT PLENTY OF **FLIGHT!**
?
?
!
!
TPP! BTHTPH THPTHPT!TTHPPTH!
THBBT
THANKS FOR THE SCRAPS, CHAPS! --OR SHOULD I SAY "**INVENTING POTENTIAL**"!
DID HE JUST **OUTWIT** ME??!
AFFIRMATIVE RESPONSE...
NO ONE CAN **EVER** KNOW ABOUT THIS!!
MEMORY WIPE ENGAGED...
KLUNK!
...SHUM DAE I GONNA BE A SCI-EN-TIST, MOMMY! HEH-HEH! HAW! HAW!
BZZT!

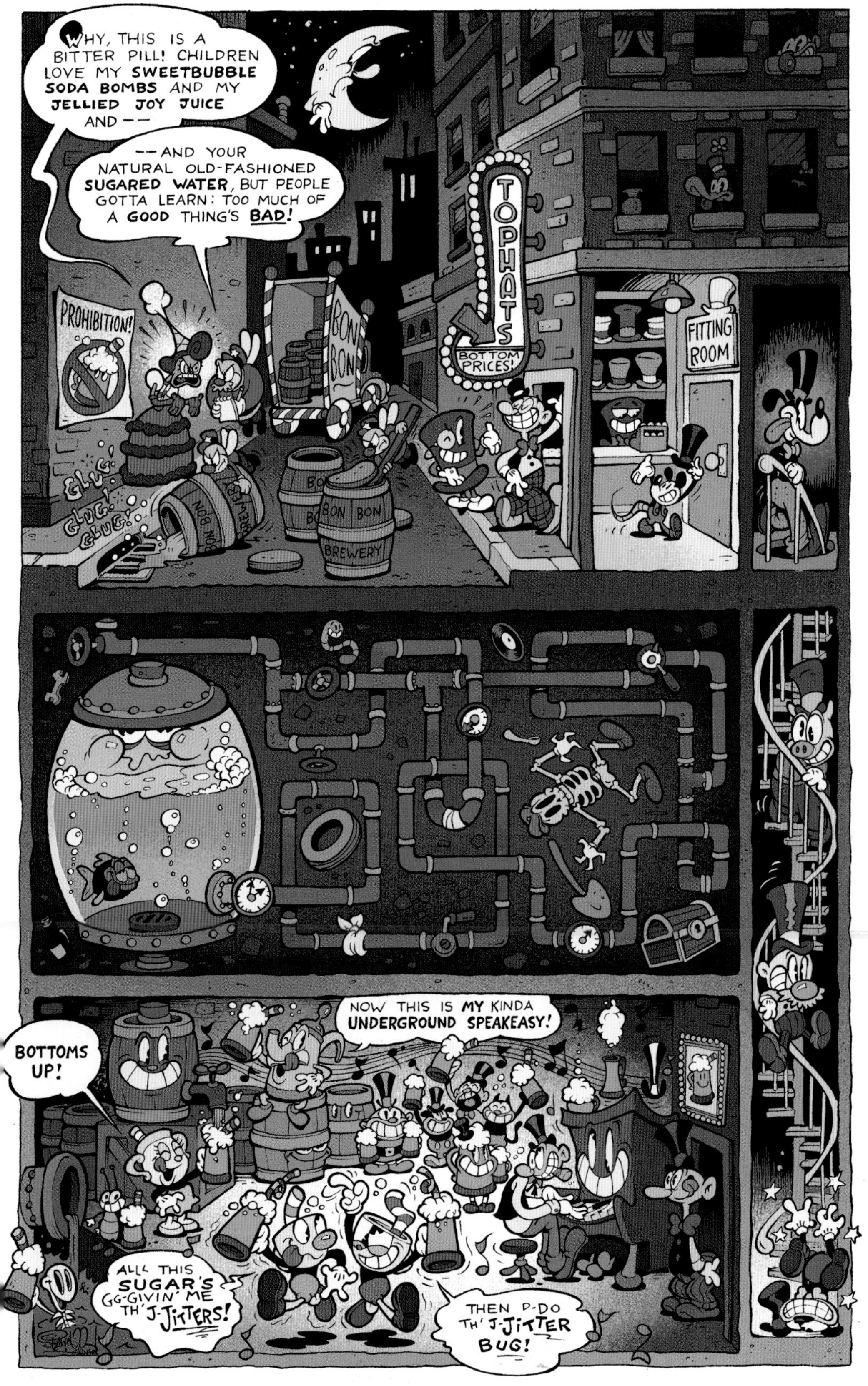
WHY, THIS IS A BITTER PILL! CHILDREN LOVE MY **SWEETBUBBLE SODA BOMBS** AND MY **JELLIED JOY JUICE** AND --
-- AND YOUR NATURAL OLD-FASHIONED **SUGARED WATER**, BUT PEOPLE GOTTA LEARN: TOO MUCH OF A **GOOD** THING'S **BAD**!
PROHIBITION!
BON BON
TOPHATS
BOTTOM PRICES!
FITTING ROOM
GLUG! GLUG! GLUG!
BON BON BREWERY
BOTTOMS UP!
NOW THIS IS **MY** KINDA **UNDERGROUND SPEAKEASY**!
ALL THIS SUGAR'S GG-GIVIN' ME TH' J-JITTERS!
THEN D-DO TH' J-JITTER BUG!

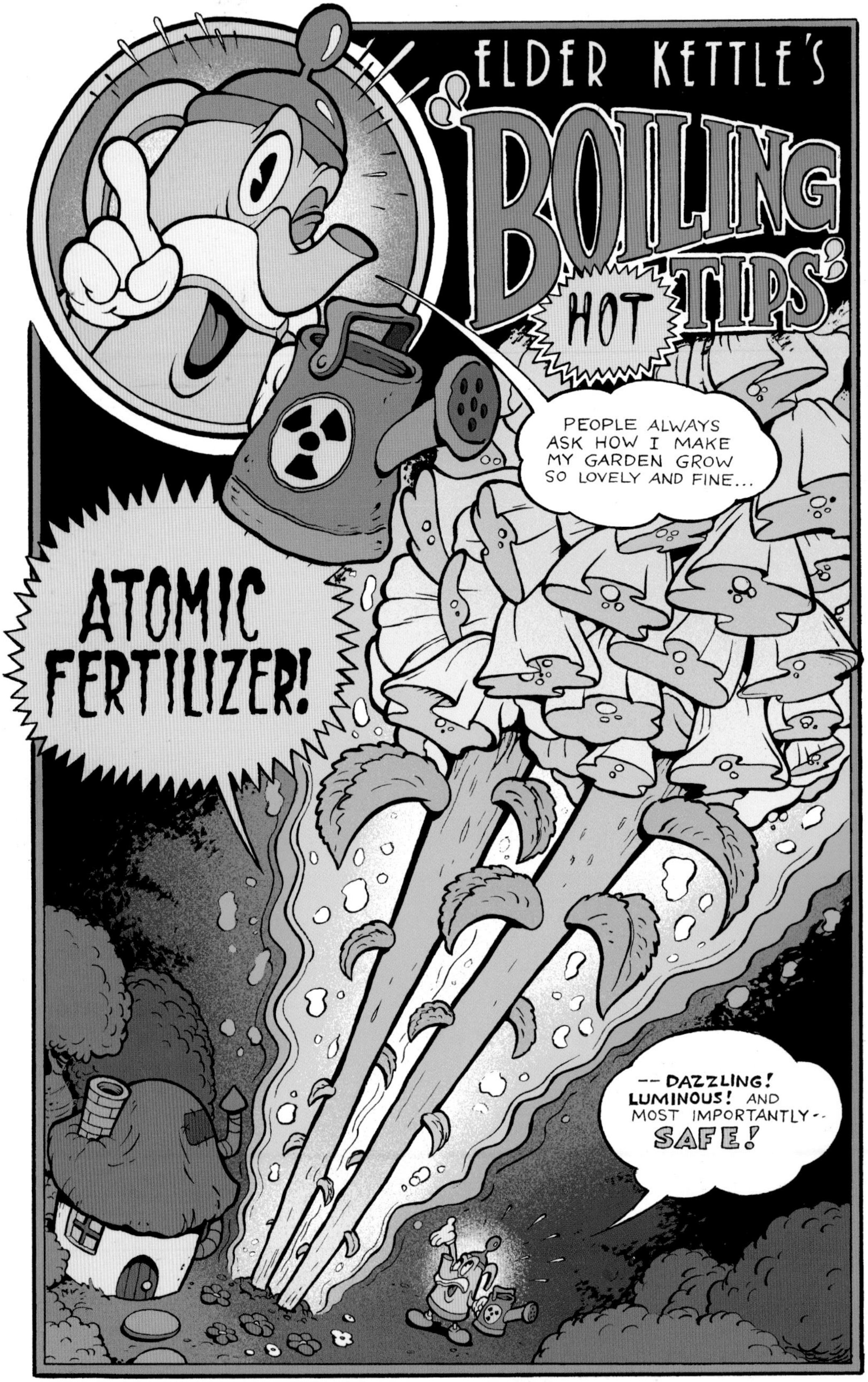

ELDER KETTLE'S
'BOILING HOT TIPS'
PEOPLE ALWAYS ASK HOW I MAKE MY GARDEN GROW SO LOVELY AND FINE...
ATOMIC FERTILIZER!
-- DAZZLING! LUMINOUS! AND MOST IMPORTANTLY -- SAFE!

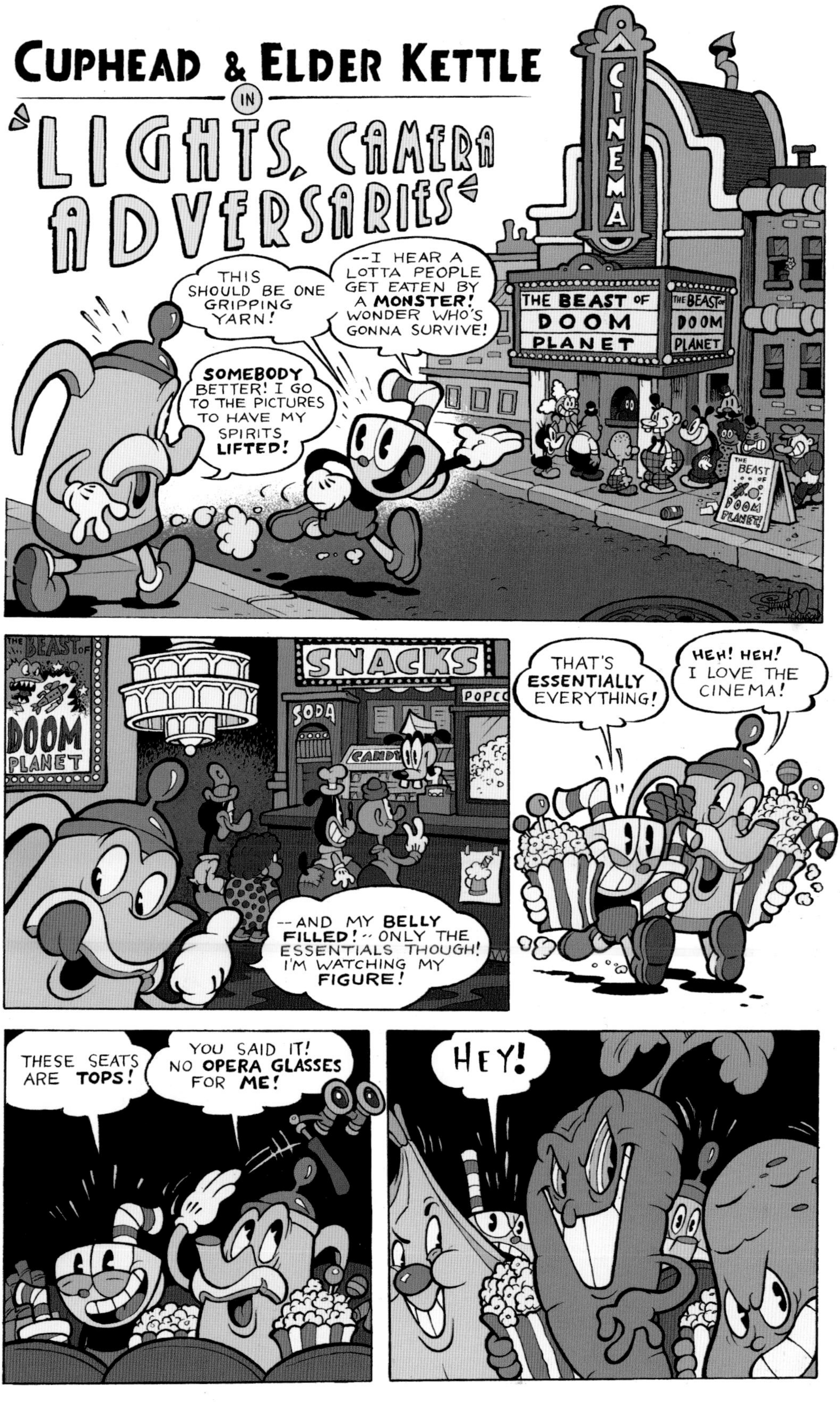
CUPHEAD & ELDER KETTLE
IN
"LIGHTS, CAMERA ADVERSARIES"
CINEMA
THE BEAST OF DOOM PLANET
THE BEAST OF DOOM PLANET
THIS SHOULD BE ONE GRIPPING YARN!
--I HEAR A LOTTA PEOPLE GET EATEN BY A **MONSTER!** WONDER WHO'S GONNA SURVIVE!
SOMEBODY BETTER! I GO TO THE PICTURES TO HAVE MY SPIRITS **LIFTED!**
THE BEAST OF DOOM PLANET!
THE BEAST OF DOOM PLANET
SNACKS
SODA
POPCO
CANDY
--AND MY **BELLY FILLED!** -- ONLY THE ESSENTIALS THOUGH! I'M WATCHING MY **FIGURE!**
THAT'S **ESSENTIALLY** EVERYTHING!
HEH! HEH! I LOVE THE CINEMA!
THESE SEATS ARE **TOPS!**
YOU SAID IT! NO **OPERA GLASSES** FOR **ME!**
HEY!

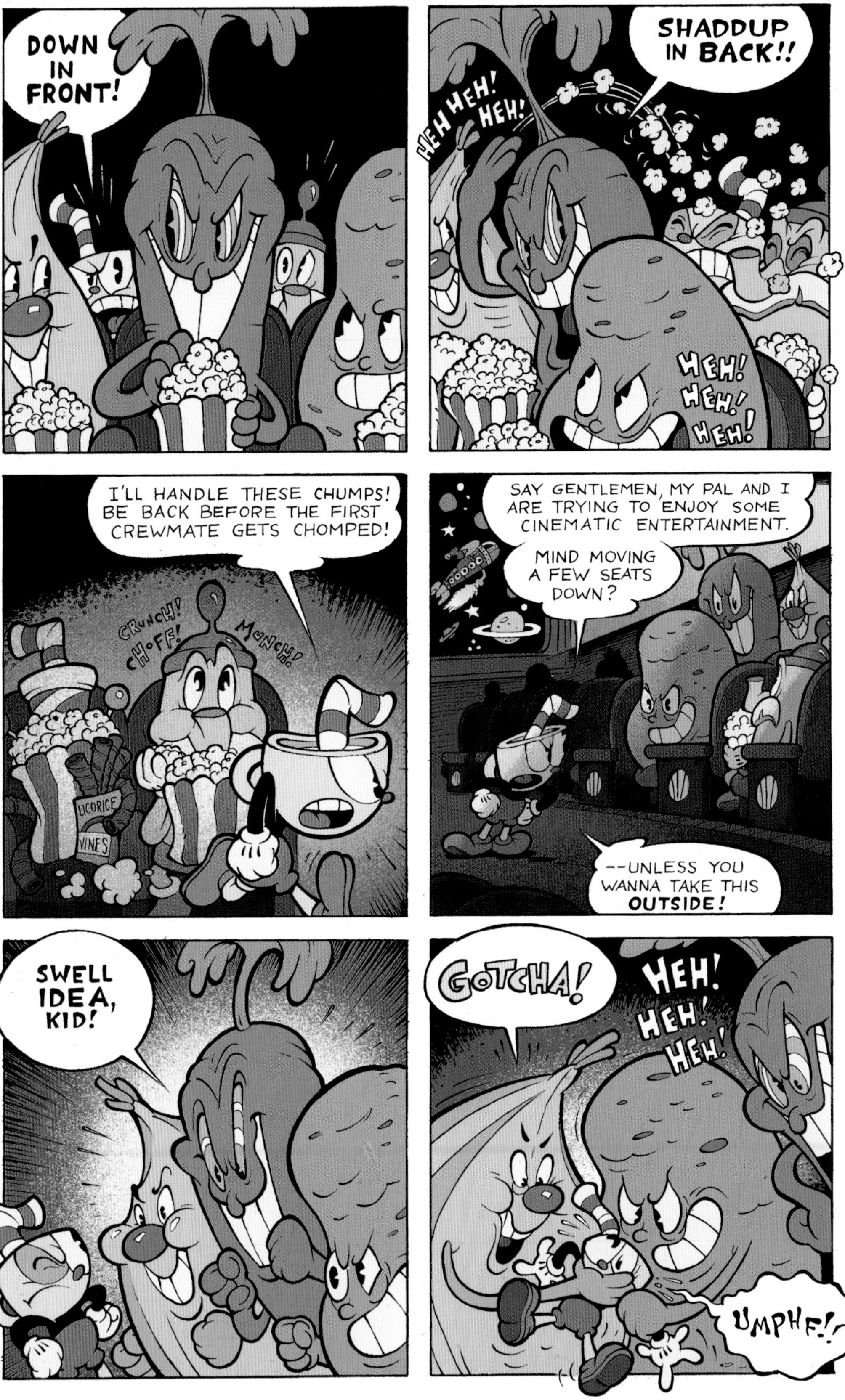
DOWN IN FRONT!
SHADDUP IN BACK!!
HEH HEH! HEH!
HEH! HEH! HEH!
I'LL HANDLE THESE CHUMPS! BE BACK BEFORE THE FIRST CREWMATE GETS CHOMPED!
CRUNCH! CHOFF!
MUNCH!
LICORICE
VINES
SAY GENTLEMEN, MY PAL AND I ARE TRYING TO ENJOY SOME CINEMATIC ENTERTAINMENT.
MIND MOVING A FEW SEATS DOWN?
--UNLESS YOU WANNA TAKE THIS OUTSIDE!
SWELL IDEA, KID!
GOTCHA!
HEH! HEH! HEH!
UMPHF!!

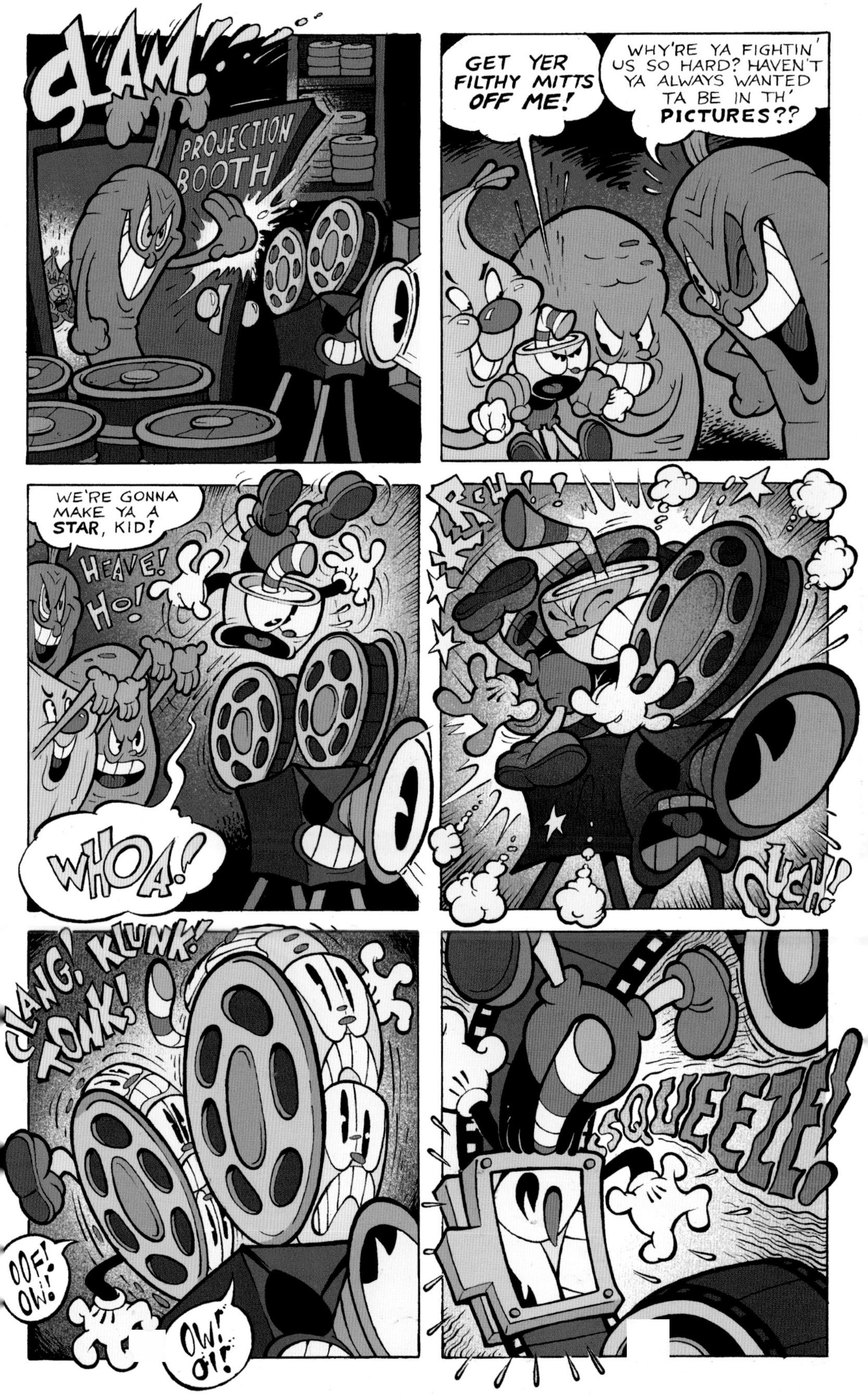
SLAM!
PROJECTION BOOTH
GET YER FILTHY MITTS OFF ME!
WHY'RE YA FIGHTIN' US SO HARD? HAVEN'T YA ALWAYS WANTED TA BE IN TH' PICTURES??
WE'RE GONNA MAKE YA A STAR, KID!
HEAVE! HO!
WHOA!
OUCH!
CLANG! KLUNK! TONK!
OOF! OW!
OW! OI!
SQUEEZE!

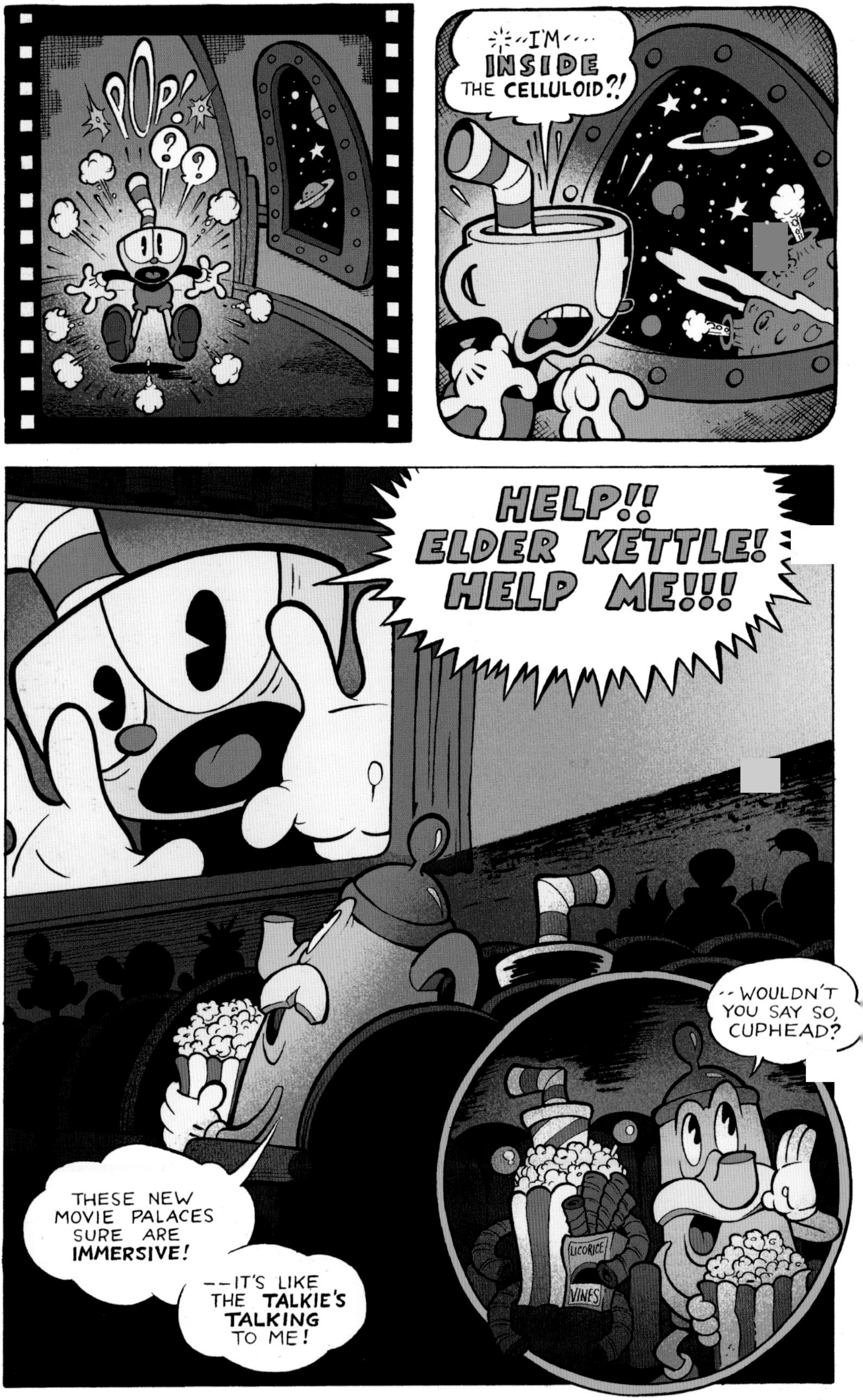
POP!
?
?
I'M INSIDE THE CELLULOID?!
HELP!! ELDER KETTLE! HELP ME!!!
THESE NEW MOVIE PALACES SURE ARE IMMERSIVE!
--IT'S LIKE THE TALKIE'S TALKING TO ME!
--WOULDN'T YOU SAY SO, CUPHEAD?
LICORICE VINES

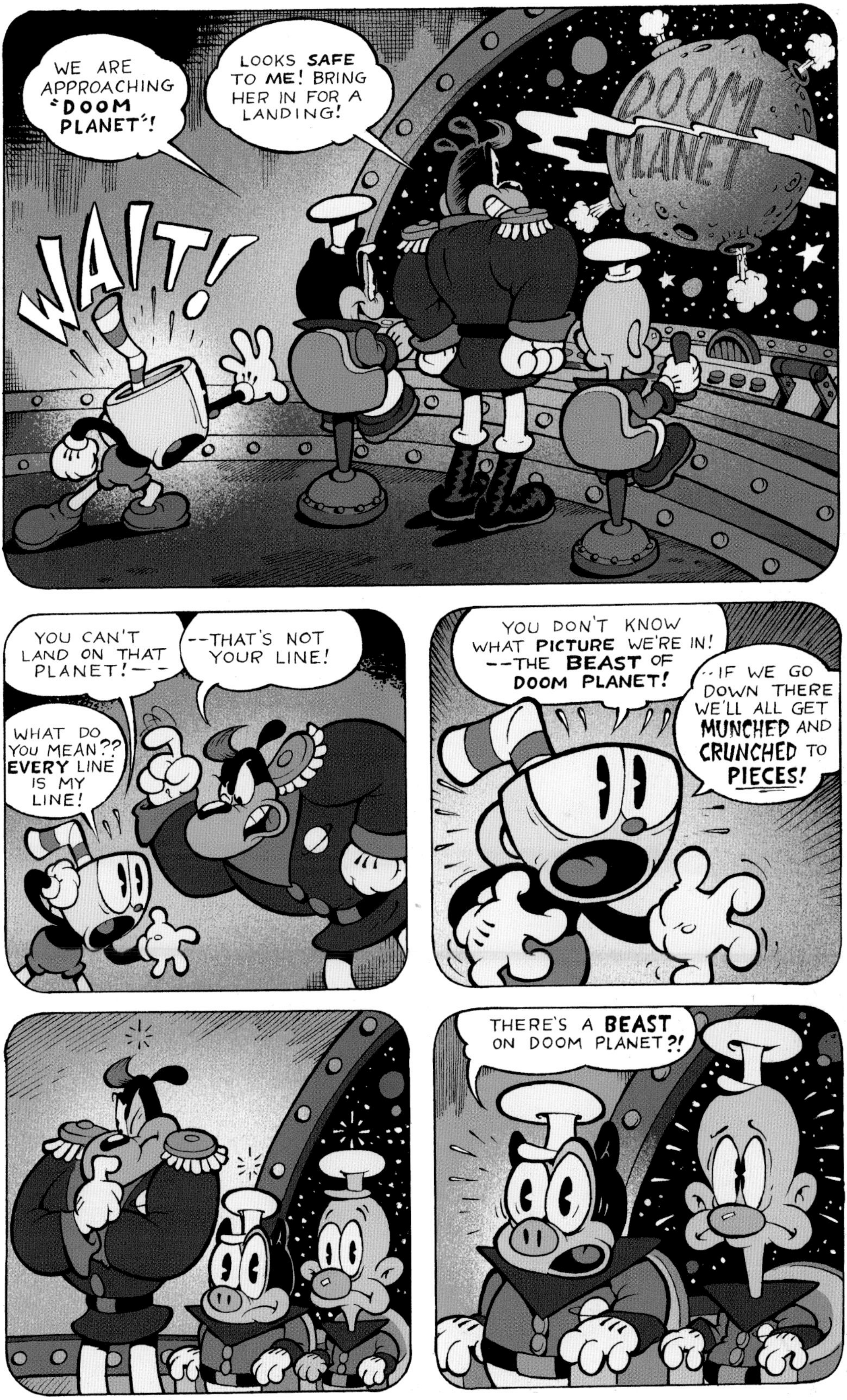
WE ARE APPROACHING "DOOM PLANET"!
LOOKS SAFE TO ME! BRING HER IN FOR A LANDING!
DOOM PLANET
WAIT!
YOU CAN'T LAND ON THAT PLANET!--
--THAT'S NOT YOUR LINE!
WHAT DO YOU MEAN?? EVERY LINE IS MY LINE!
YOU DON'T KNOW WHAT PICTURE WE'RE IN! --THE BEAST OF DOOM PLANET!
--IF WE GO DOWN THERE WE'LL ALL GET MUNCHED AND CRUNCHED TO PIECES!
THERE'S A BEAST ON DOOM PLANET?!

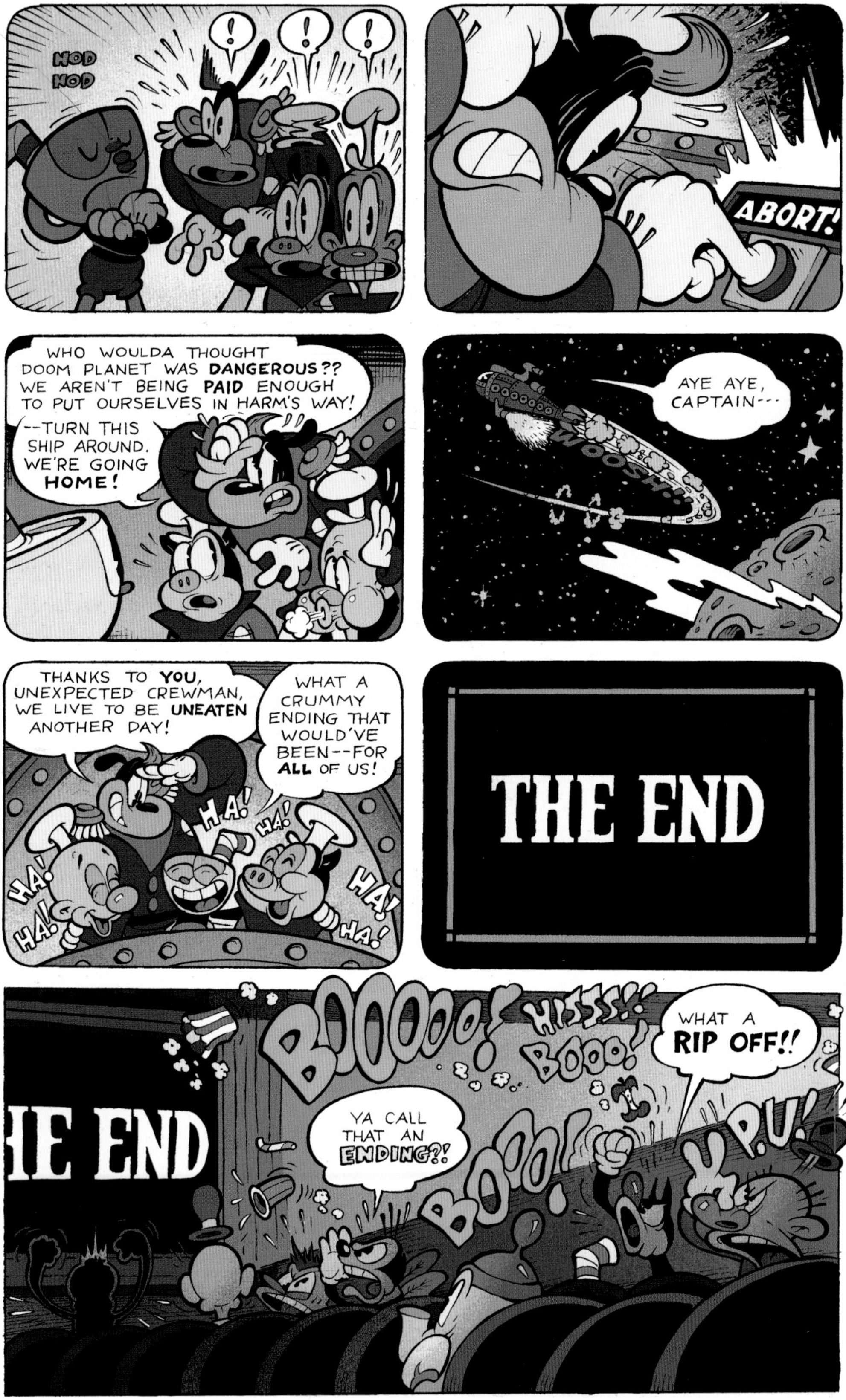
NOD NOD
!
!
!
ABORT!
WHO WOULDA THOUGHT DOOM PLANET WAS DANGEROUS?? WE AREN'T BEING PAID ENOUGH TO PUT OURSELVES IN HARM'S WAY!
--TURN THIS SHIP AROUND. WE'RE GOING HOME!
AYE AYE, CAPTAIN---
WOOSH
THANKS TO YOU, UNEXPECTED CREWMAN, WE LIVE TO BE UNEATEN ANOTHER DAY!
WHAT A CRUMMY ENDING THAT WOULD'VE BEEN--FOR ALL OF US!
HA! HA! HA! HA! HA! HA! HA!
THE END
BOOOOO! HISSS!! BOOO!
WHAT A RIP OFF!!
HE END
YA CALL THAT AN ENDING?!
BOOO!
P.U.!

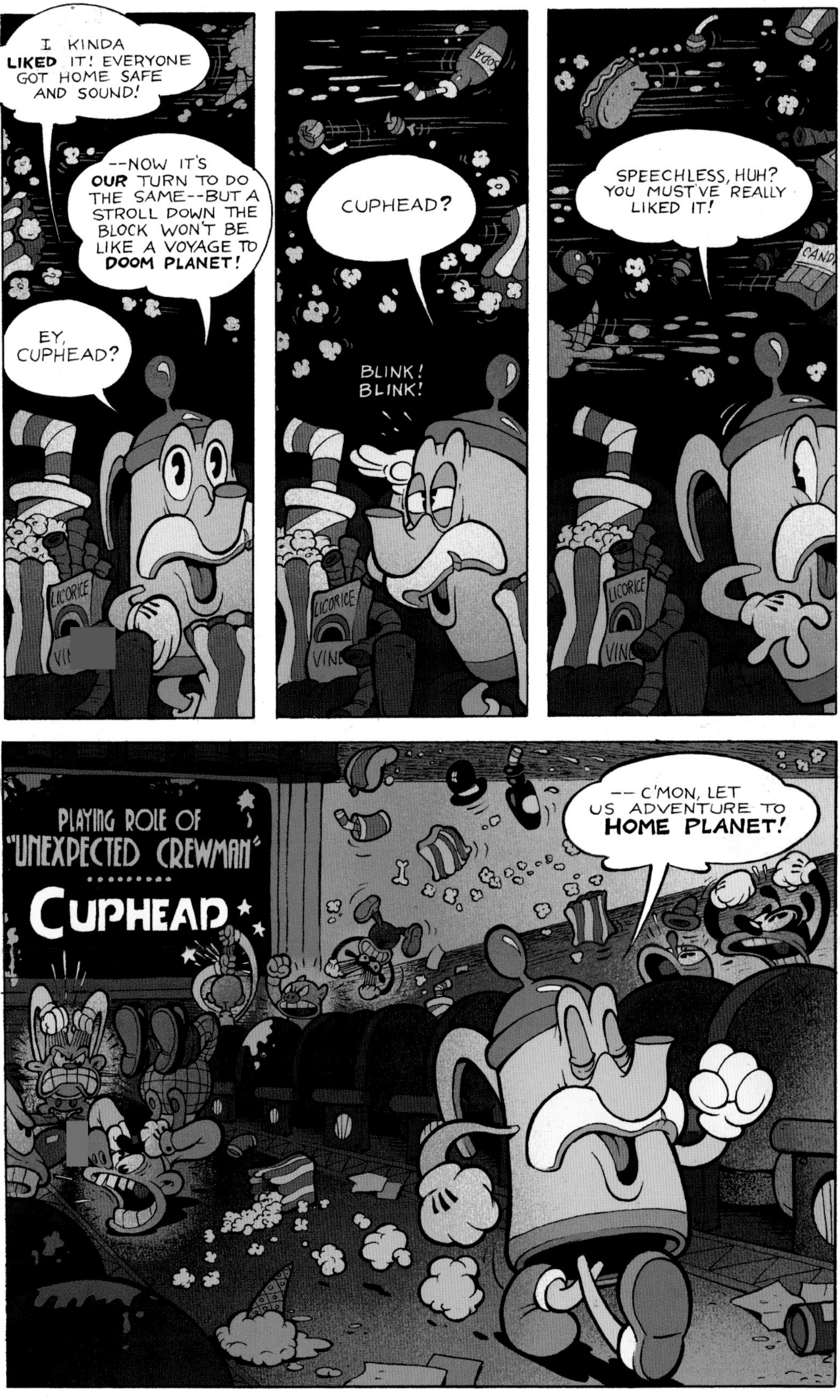
I KINDA LIKED IT! EVERYONE GOT HOME SAFE AND SOUND!
--NOW IT'S OUR TURN TO DO THE SAME--BUT A STROLL DOWN THE BLOCK WON'T BE LIKE A VOYAGE TO DOOM PLANET!
EY, CUPHEAD?
LICORICE
SODA
CUPHEAD?
BLINK! BLINK!
LICORICE
SPEECHLESS, HUH? YOU MUST'VE REALLY LIKED IT!
LICORICE
PLAYING ROLE OF "UNEXPECTED CREWMAN"
CUPHEAD
-- C'MON, LET US ADVENTURE TO HOME PLANET!

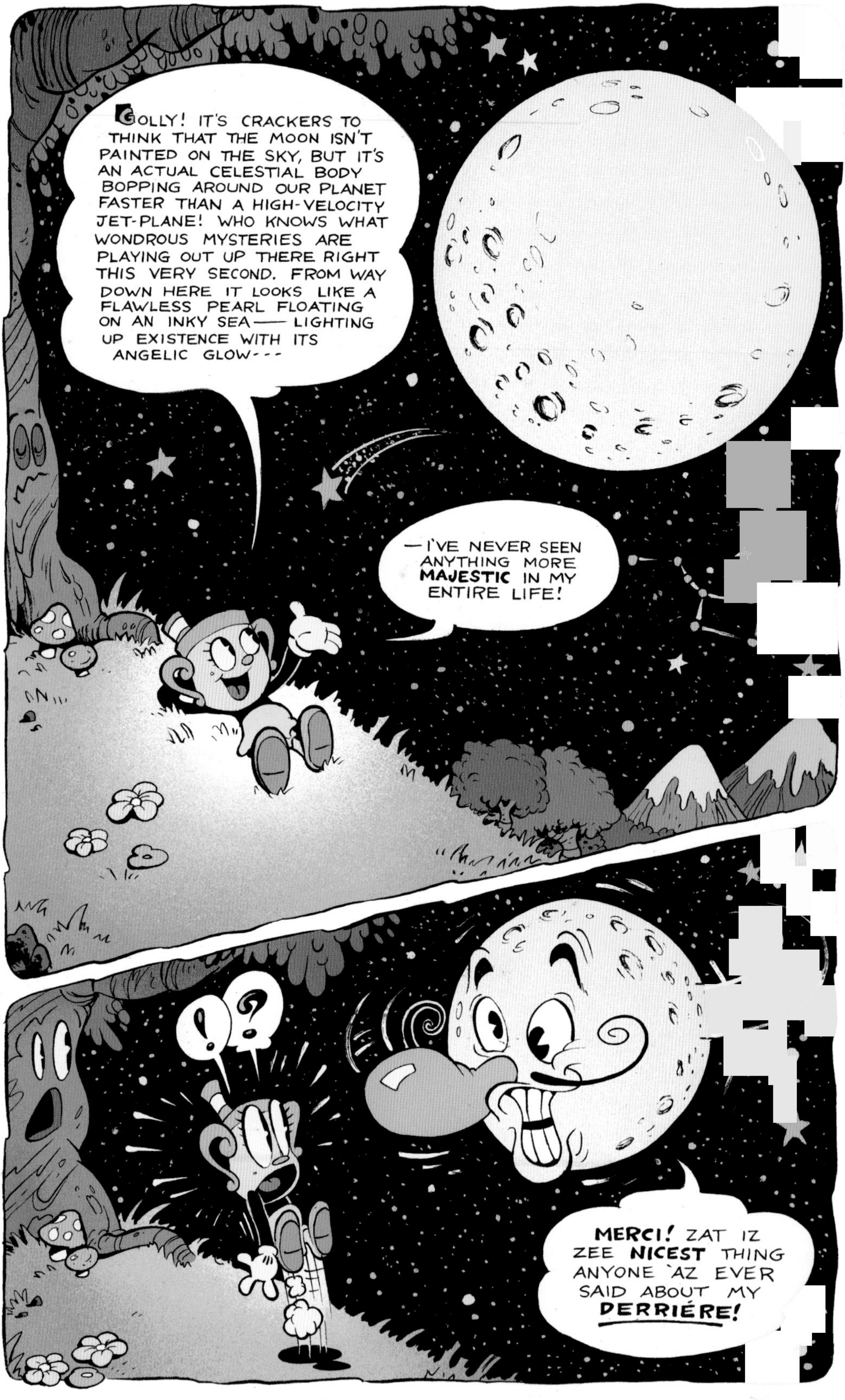
GOLLY! IT'S CRACKERS TO THINK THAT THE MOON ISN'T PAINTED ON THE SKY, BUT IT'S AN ACTUAL CELESTIAL BODY BOPPING AROUND OUR PLANET FASTER THAN A HIGH-VELOCITY JET-PLANE! WHO KNOWS WHAT WONDROUS MYSTERIES ARE PLAYING OUT UP THERE RIGHT THIS VERY SECOND. FROM WAY DOWN HERE IT LOOKS LIKE A FLAWLESS PEARL FLOATING ON AN INKY SEA— LIGHTING UP EXISTENCE WITH ITS ANGELIC GLOW---
—I'VE NEVER SEEN ANYTHING MORE MAJESTIC IN MY ENTIRE LIFE!
MERCI! ZAT IZ ZEE NICEST THING ANYONE `AZ EVER SAID ABOUT MY DERRIÉRE!

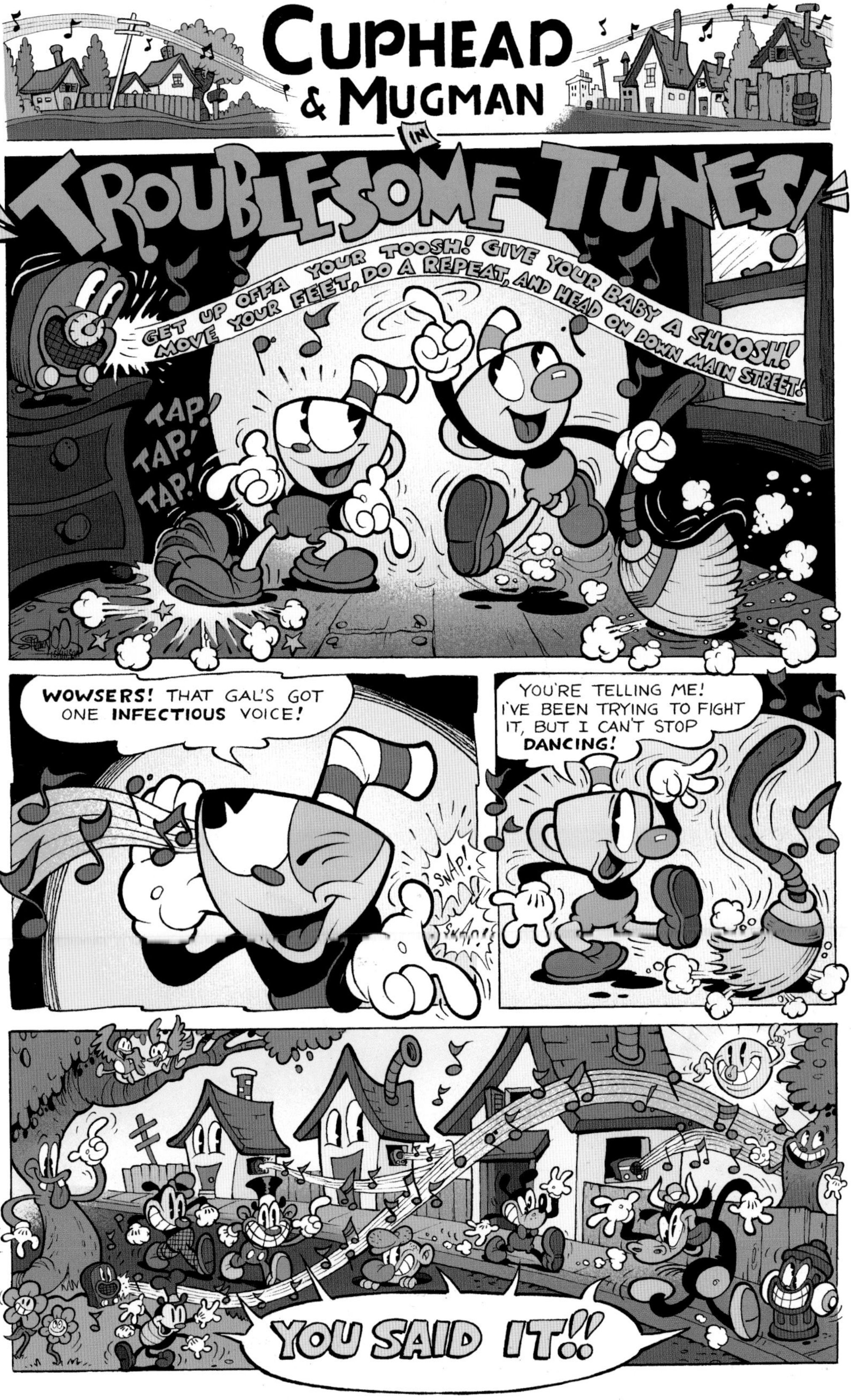
CUPHEAD & MUGMAN
IN
TROUBLESOME TUNES!
GET UP OFFA YOUR TOOSH! GIVE YOUR BABY A SHOOSH! MOVE YOUR FEET, DO A REPEAT, AND HEAD ON DOWN MAIN STREET!
TAP! TAP! TAP!
WOWSERS! THAT GAL'S GOT ONE INFECTIOUS VOICE!
SNAP!
YOU'RE TELLING ME! I'VE BEEN TRYING TO FIGHT IT, BUT I CAN'T STOP DANCING!
YOU SAID IT!!

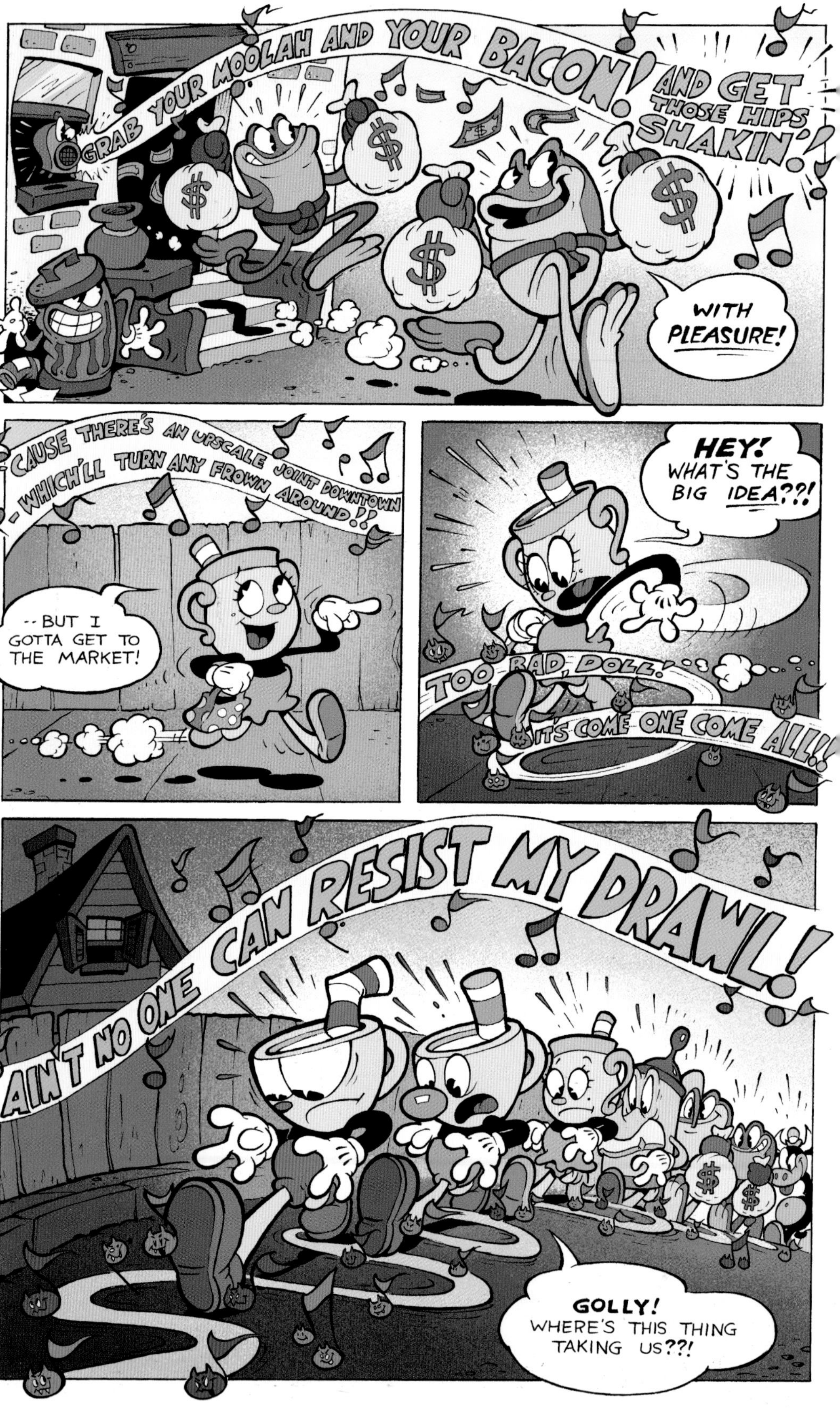
GRAB YOUR MOOLAH AND YOUR BACON! AND GET THOSE HIPS SHAKIN'!
WITH PLEASURE!
'CAUSE THERE'S AN UPSCALE JOINT DOWNTOWN -WHICH'LL TURN ANY FROWN AROUND!!
--BUT I GOTTA GET TO THE MARKET!
HEY! WHAT'S THE BIG IDEA??!
TOO BAD, DOLL!
IT'S COME ONE COME ALL!!
AIN'T NO ONE CAN RESIST MY DRAWL!
GOLLY! WHERE'S THIS THING TAKING US??!

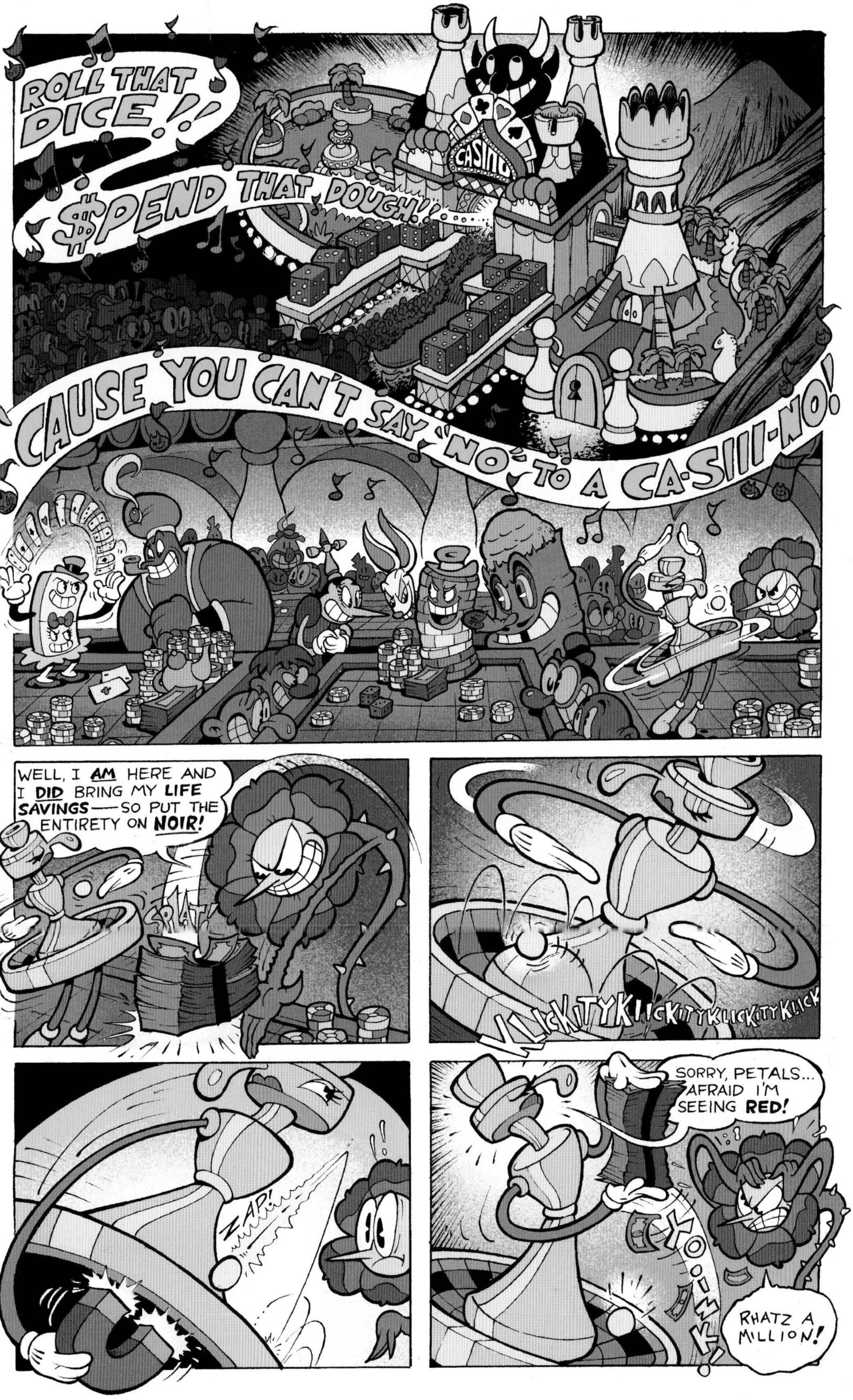
ROLL THAT DICE!!
$PEND THAT DOUGH!!
CASINO
CAUSE YOU CAN'T SAY "NO" TO A CA-SIII-NO!
WELL, I AM HERE AND I DID BRING MY LIFE SAVINGS—SO PUT THE ENTIRETY ON NOIR!
SPLAT!
KLICKITYKLICKITYKLICKITYKLICKITYKLICK
ZAP!
SORRY, PETALS... AFRAID I'M SEEING RED!
KOOINK!
RHATZ A MILLION!

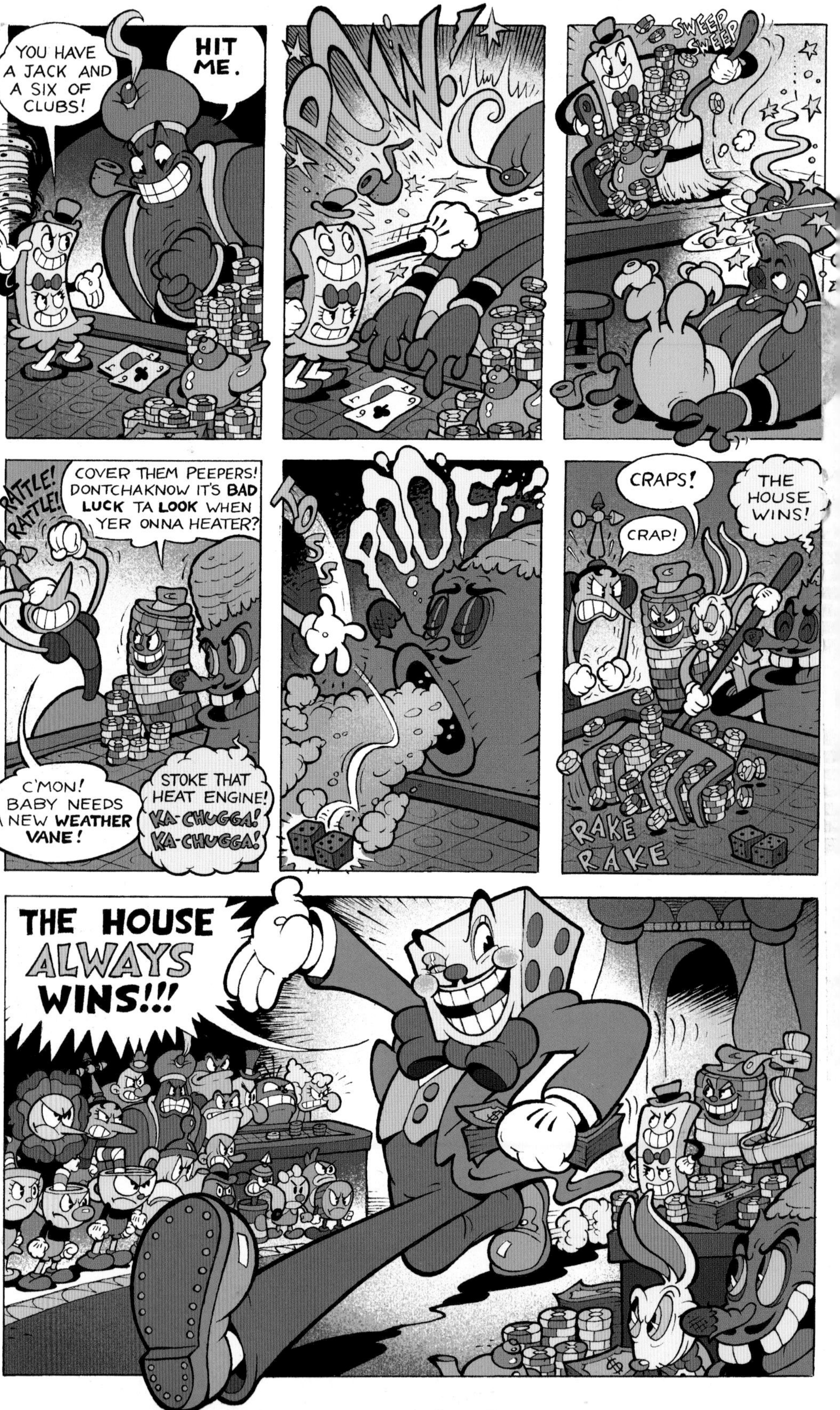
YOU HAVE A JACK AND A SIX OF CLUBS!
HIT ME.
POW!
SWEEP SWEEP
RATTLE! RATTLE!
COVER THEM PEEPERS! DONTCHAKNOW IT'S BAD LUCK TA LOOK WHEN YER ONNA HEATER?
C'MON! BABY NEEDS A NEW WEATHER VANE!
STOKE THAT HEAT ENGINE! KA-CHUGGA! KA-CHUGGA!
TOSS
POOF!
CRAPS!
CRAP!
THE HOUSE WINS!
RAKE RAKE
THE HOUSE ALWAYS WINS!!!

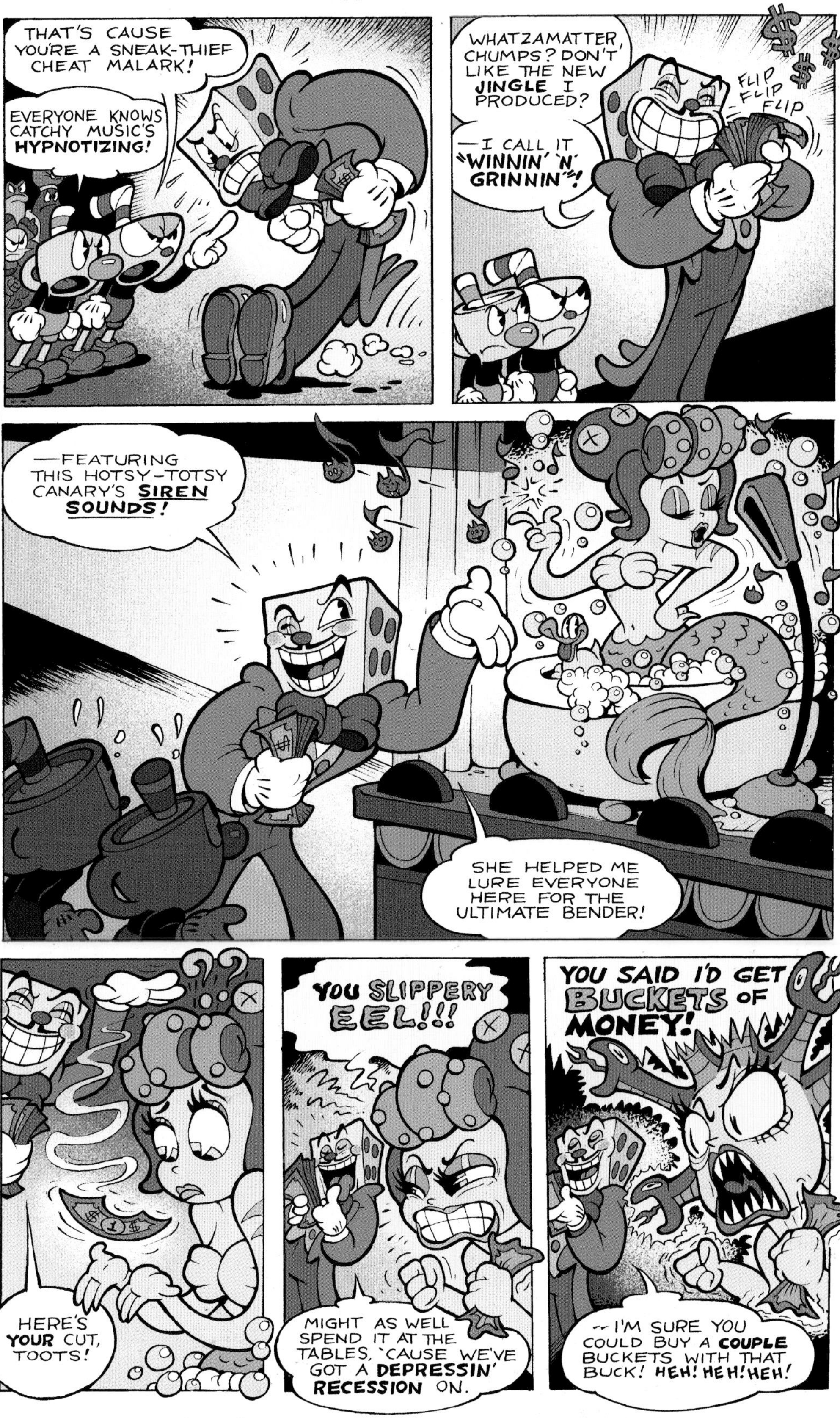
THAT'S CAUSE YOU'RE A SNEAK-THIEF CHEAT MALARK!
EVERYONE KNOWS CATCHY MUSIC'S **HYPNOTIZING**!
WHATZAMATTER, CHUMPS? DON'T LIKE THE NEW **JINGLE** I PRODUCED?
FLIP FLIP FLIP
—I CALL IT "**WINNIN' 'N' GRINNIN'**"!
—FEATURING THIS HOTSY-TOTSY CANARY'S **SIREN SOUNDS**!
SHE HELPED ME LURE EVERYONE HERE FOR THE ULTIMATE BENDER!
HERE'S **YOUR** CUT, TOOTS!
YOU SLIPPERY EEL!!!
MIGHT AS WELL SPEND IT AT THE TABLES, 'CAUSE WE'VE GOT A **DEPRESSIN' RECESSION** ON.
YOU SAID I'D GET BUCKETS OF MONEY!
--I'M SURE YOU COULD BUY A **COUPLE** BUCKETS WITH THAT BUCK! **HEH! HEH! HEH!**

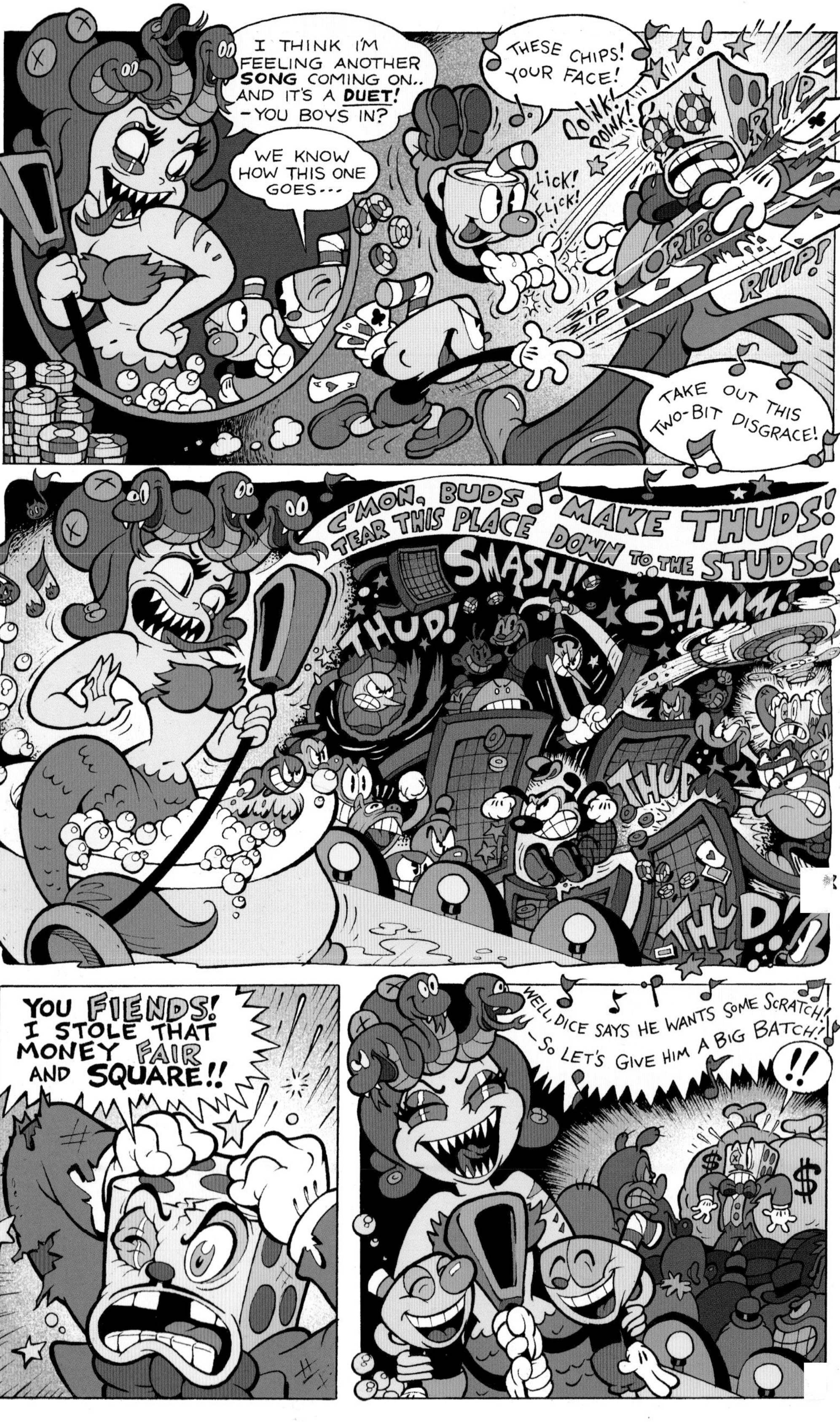
I THINK I'M FEELING ANOTHER SONG COMING ON.. AND IT'S A DUET! -YOU BOYS IN?
WE KNOW HOW THIS ONE GOES---
THESE CHIPS! YOUR FACE!
POINK! POINK!
FLICK! FLICK!
RIIIP!
RIP!
RIIIP!
ZIP ZIP
TAKE OUT THIS TWO-BIT DISGRACE!
C'MON, BUDS TEAR THIS PLACE
MAKE THUDS! DOWN TO THE STUDS!
SMASH!
THUD!
SLAMM!
THUD
THUD!
YOU FIENDS! I STOLE THAT MONEY FAIR AND SQUARE!!
WELL, DICE SAYS HE WANTS SOME SCRATCH!
-SO LET'S GIVE HIM A BIG BATCH!
!!

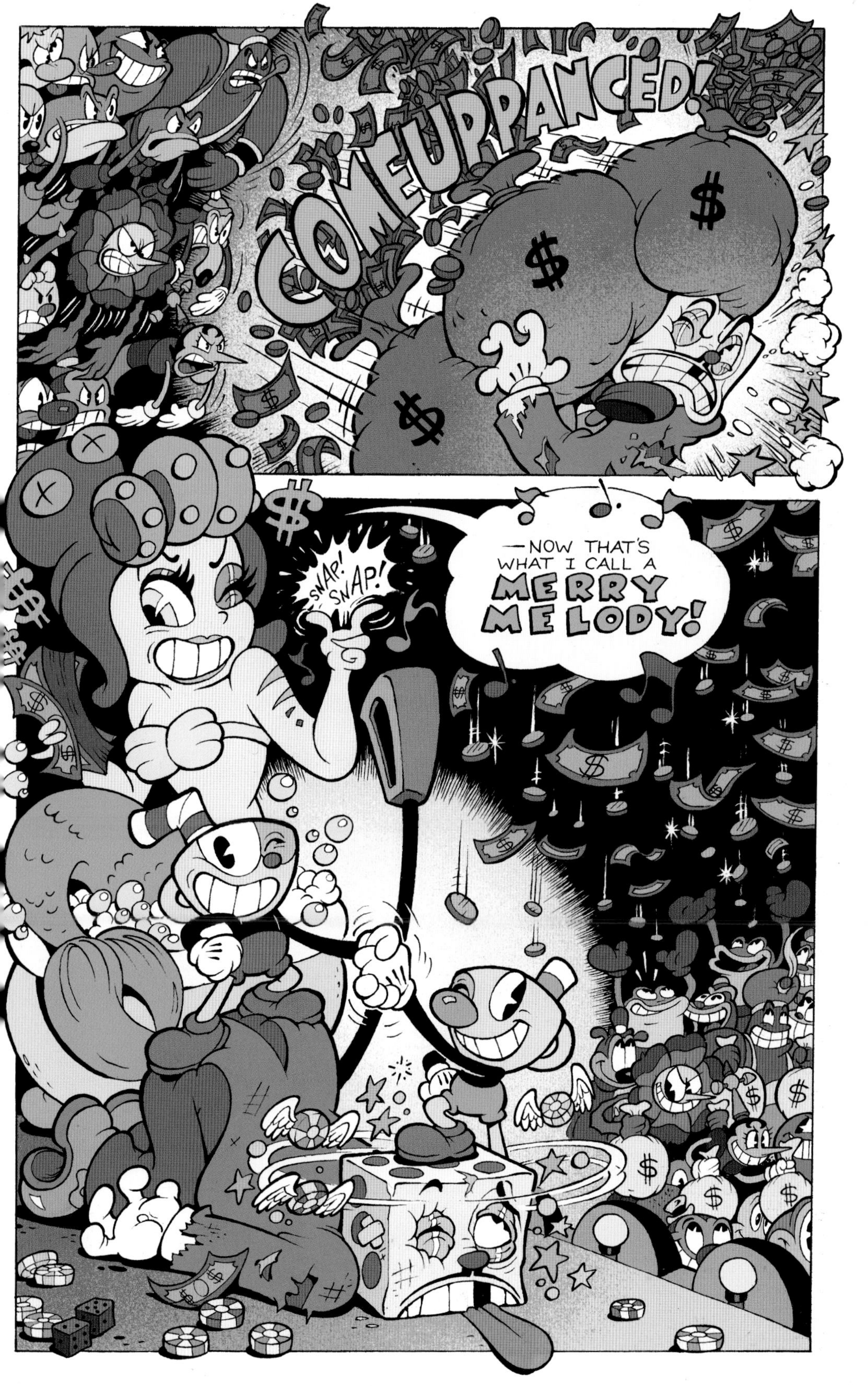
COMEUPPANCED!
SNAP! SNAP!
—NOW THAT'S WHAT I CALL A MERRY MELODY!

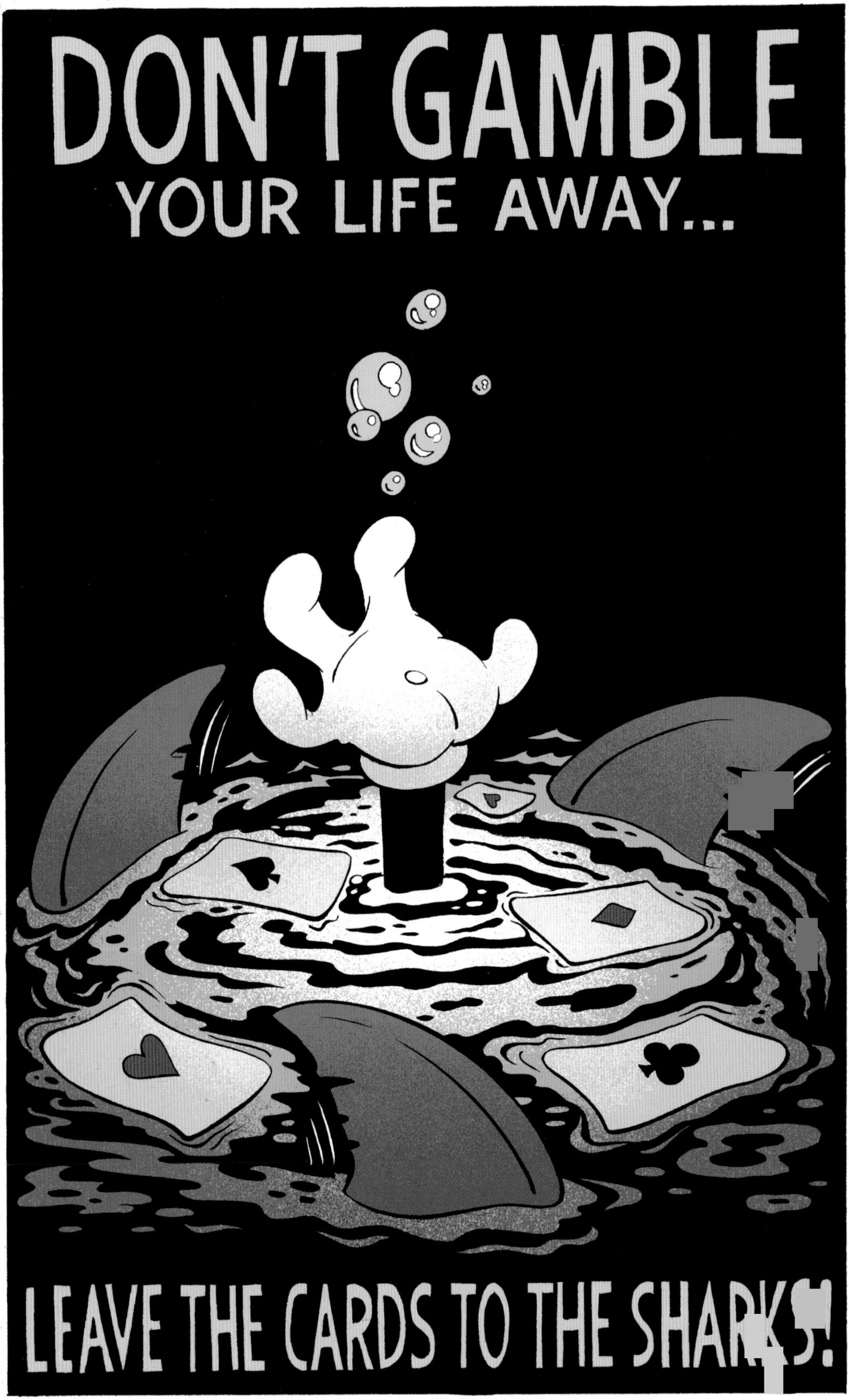
DON'T GAMBLE
YOUR LIFE AWAY...
LEAVE THE CARDS TO THE SHARKS!

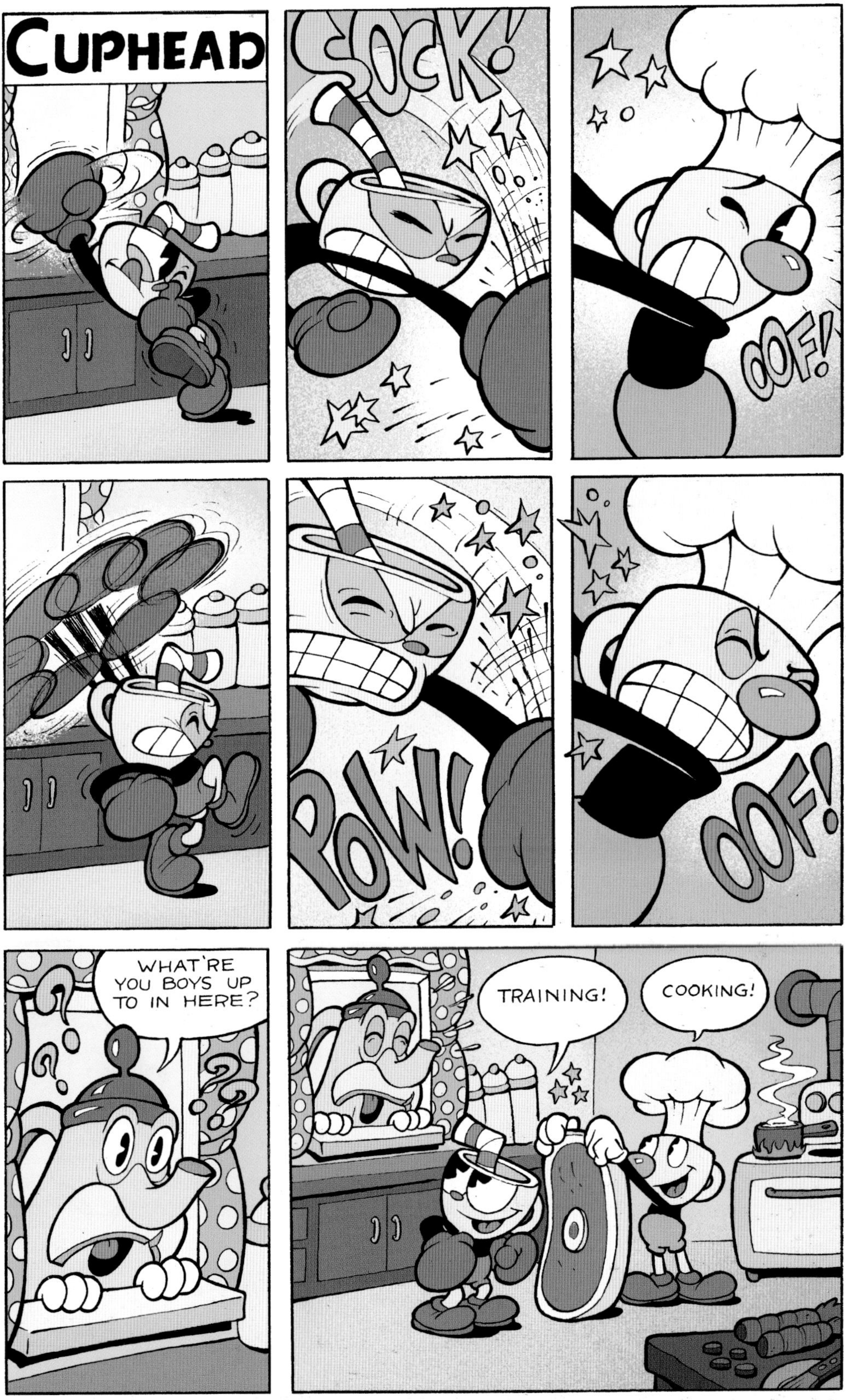
CUPHEAD
SOCK!
OOF!
POW!
OOF!
WHAT'RE YOU BOYS UP TO IN HERE?
TRAINING!
COOKING!

HOW TO BE A STRAPPING SCRAPPER: FROM NOODLE-ARM NINNY TO NOGGIN KNOCKER!

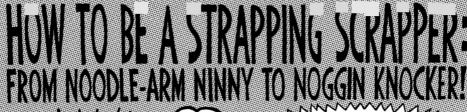

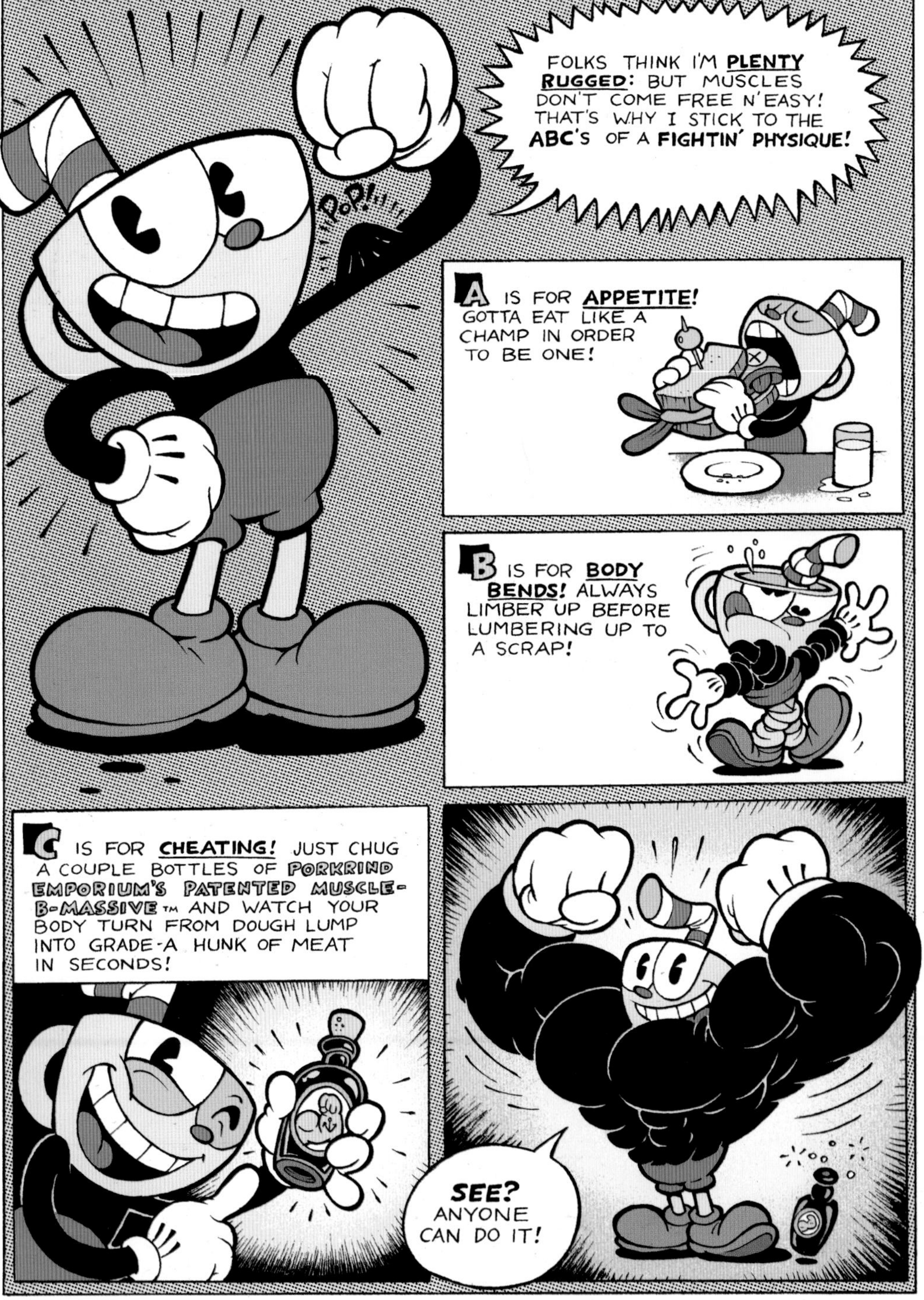
FOLKS THINK I'M PLENTY RUGGED: BUT MUSCLES DON'T COME FREE N'EASY! THAT'S WHY I STICK TO THE ABC'S OF A FIGHTIN' PHYSIQUE!
POP!
A IS FOR APPETITE! GOTTA EAT LIKE A CHAMP IN ORDER TO BE ONE!
B IS FOR BODY BENDS! ALWAYS LIMBER UP BEFORE LUMBERING UP TO A SCRAP!
C IS FOR CHEATING! JUST CHUG A COUPLE BOTTLES OF PORKRIND EMPORIUM'S PATENTED MUSCLE-B-MASSIVE™ AND WATCH YOUR BODY TURN FROM DOUGH LUMP INTO GRADE-A HUNK OF MEAT IN SECONDS!
SEE? ANYONE CAN DO IT!

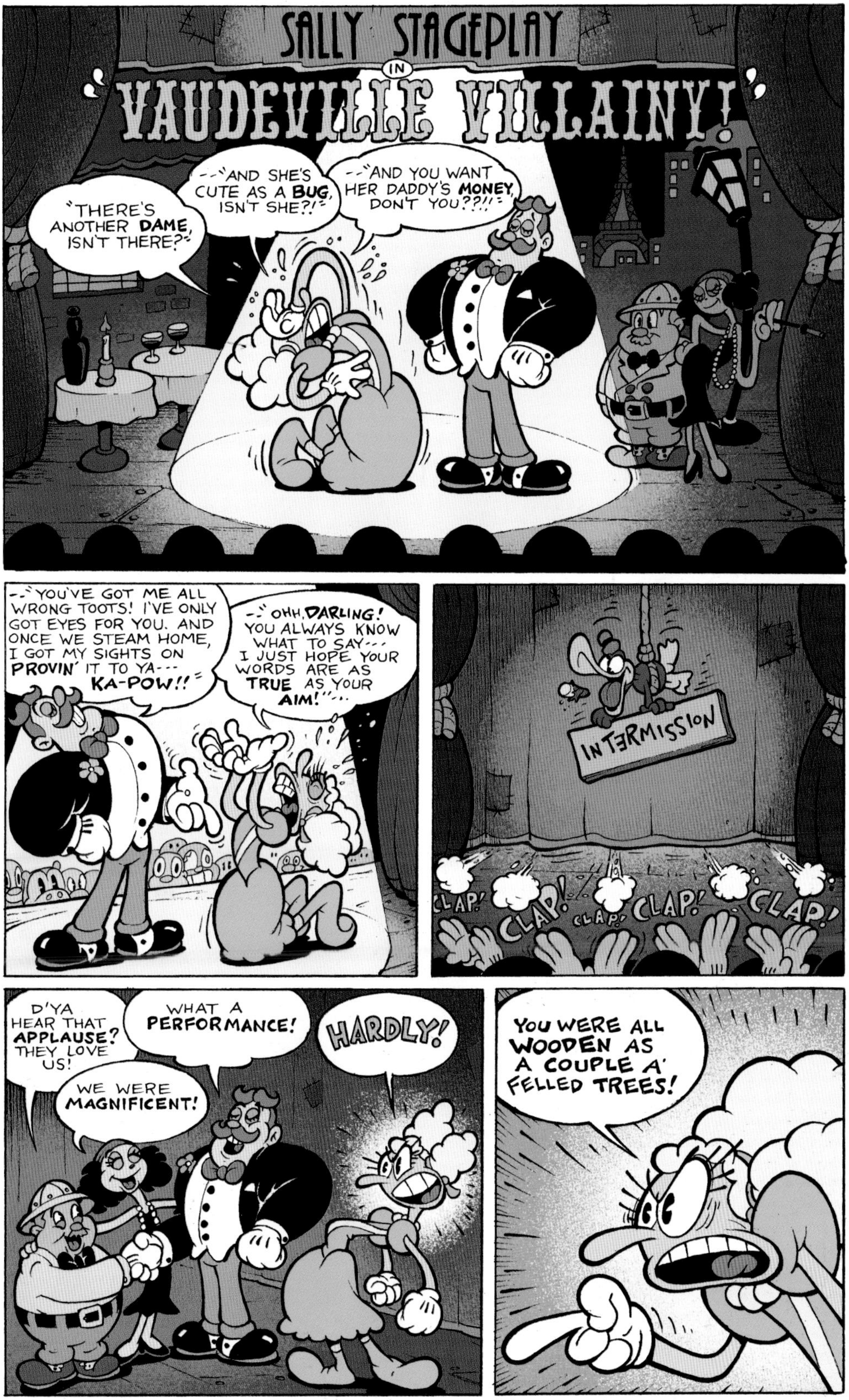
SALLY STAGEPLAY
IN
VAUDEVILLE VILLAINY!
"THERE'S ANOTHER DAME, ISN'T THERE?"
--"AND SHE'S CUTE AS A BUG, ISN'T SHE?!"
--"AND YOU WANT HER DADDY'S MONEY, DON'T YOU??!!"
--"YOU'VE GOT ME ALL WRONG TOOTS! I'VE ONLY GOT EYES FOR YOU. AND ONCE WE STEAM HOME, I GOT MY SIGHTS ON PROVIN' IT TO YA--- KA-POW!!"
--"OHH, DARLING! YOU ALWAYS KNOW WHAT TO SAY--- I JUST HOPE YOUR WORDS ARE AS TRUE AS YOUR AIM!"...
INTERMISSION
CLAP! CLAP! CLAP! CLAP! CLAP!
D'YA HEAR THAT APPLAUSE? THEY LOVE US!
WHAT A PERFORMANCE!
WE WERE MAGNIFICENT!
HARDLY!
YOU WERE ALL WOODEN AS A COUPLE A' FELLED TREES!

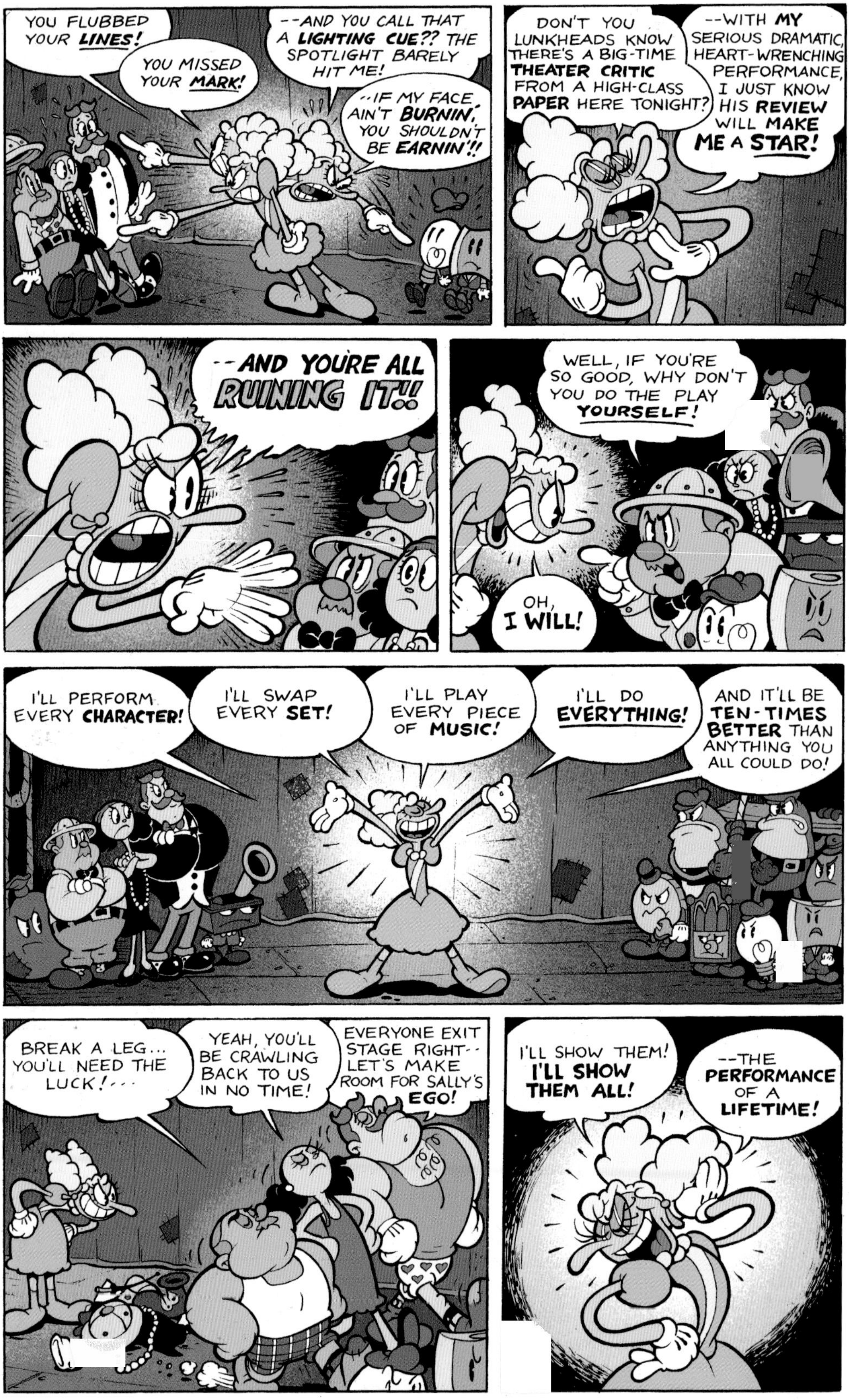
YOU FLUBBED YOUR LINES!
YOU MISSED YOUR MARK!
--AND YOU CALL THAT A LIGHTING CUE?? THE SPOTLIGHT BARELY HIT ME!
--IF MY FACE AIN'T BURNIN', YOU SHOULDN'T BE EARNIN'!!
DON'T YOU LUNKHEADS KNOW THERE'S A BIG-TIME THEATER CRITIC FROM A HIGH-CLASS PAPER HERE TONIGHT?
--WITH MY SERIOUS DRAMATIC, HEART-WRENCHING PERFORMANCE, I JUST KNOW HIS REVIEW WILL MAKE ME A STAR!
--AND YOU'RE ALL RUINING IT!!
WELL, IF YOU'RE SO GOOD, WHY DON'T YOU DO THE PLAY YOURSELF!
OH, I WILL!
I'LL PERFORM EVERY CHARACTER!
I'LL SWAP EVERY SET!
I'LL PLAY EVERY PIECE OF MUSIC!
I'LL DO EVERYTHING!
AND IT'LL BE TEN-TIMES BETTER THAN ANYTHING YOU ALL COULD DO!
BREAK A LEG... YOU'LL NEED THE LUCK!...
YEAH, YOU'LL BE CRAWLING BACK TO US IN NO TIME!
EVERYONE EXIT STAGE RIGHT-- LET'S MAKE ROOM FOR SALLY'S EGO!
I'LL SHOW THEM! I'LL SHOW THEM ALL!
--THE PERFORMANCE OF A LIFETIME!

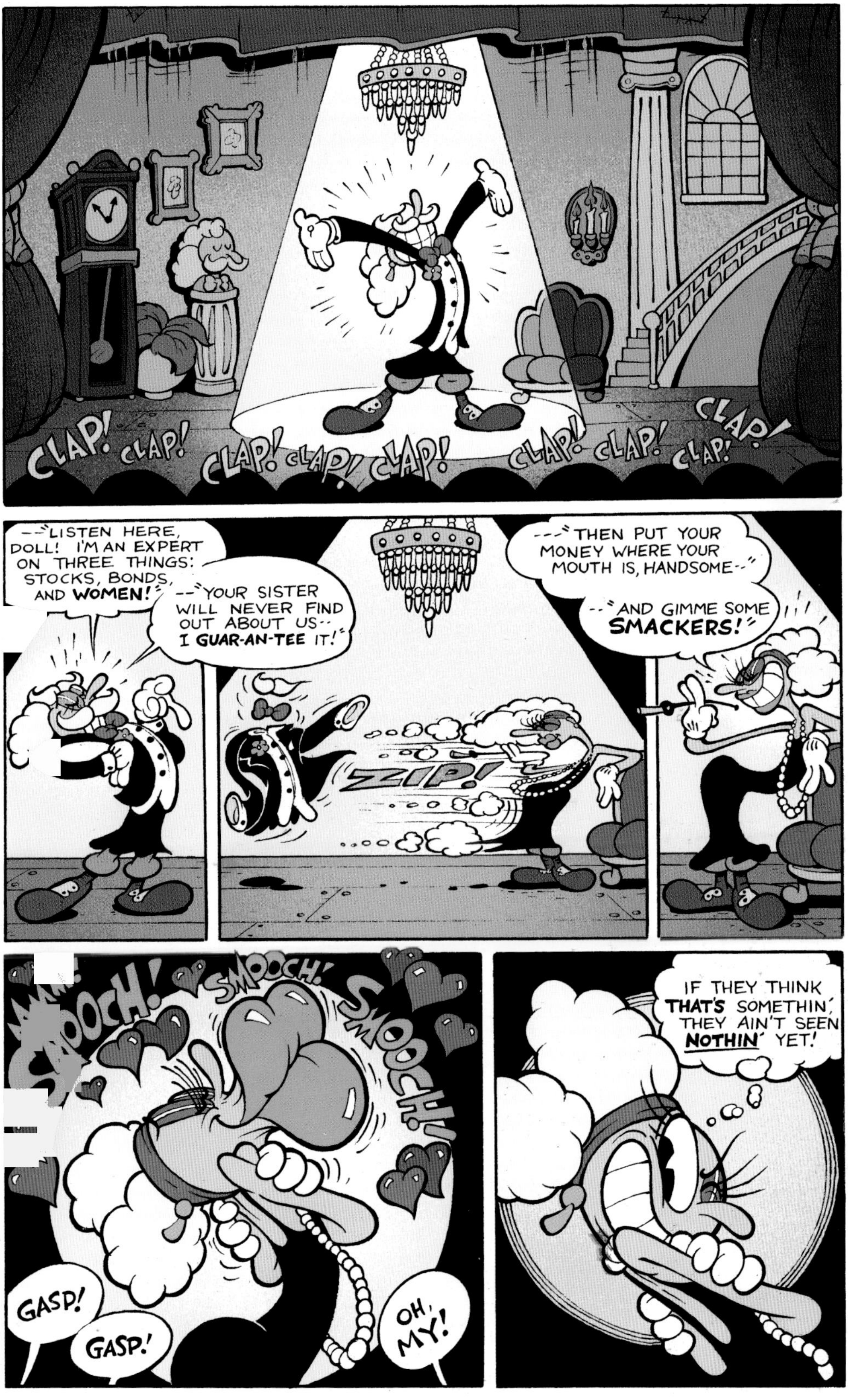
CLAP! CLAP! CLAP! CLAP! CLAP! CLAP! CLAP! CLAP! CLAP!
--LISTEN HERE, DOLL! I'M AN EXPERT ON THREE THINGS: STOCKS, BONDS, AND WOMEN!
--YOUR SISTER WILL NEVER FIND OUT ABOUT US-- I GUAR-AN-TEE IT!
--THEN PUT YOUR MONEY WHERE YOUR MOUTH IS, HANDSOME--
--AND GIMME SOME SMACKERS!
ZIP!
SMOOCH! SMOOCH! SMOOCH!
GASP! GASP!
OH, MY!
IF THEY THINK THAT'S SOMETHIN', THEY AIN'T SEEN NOTHIN' YET!

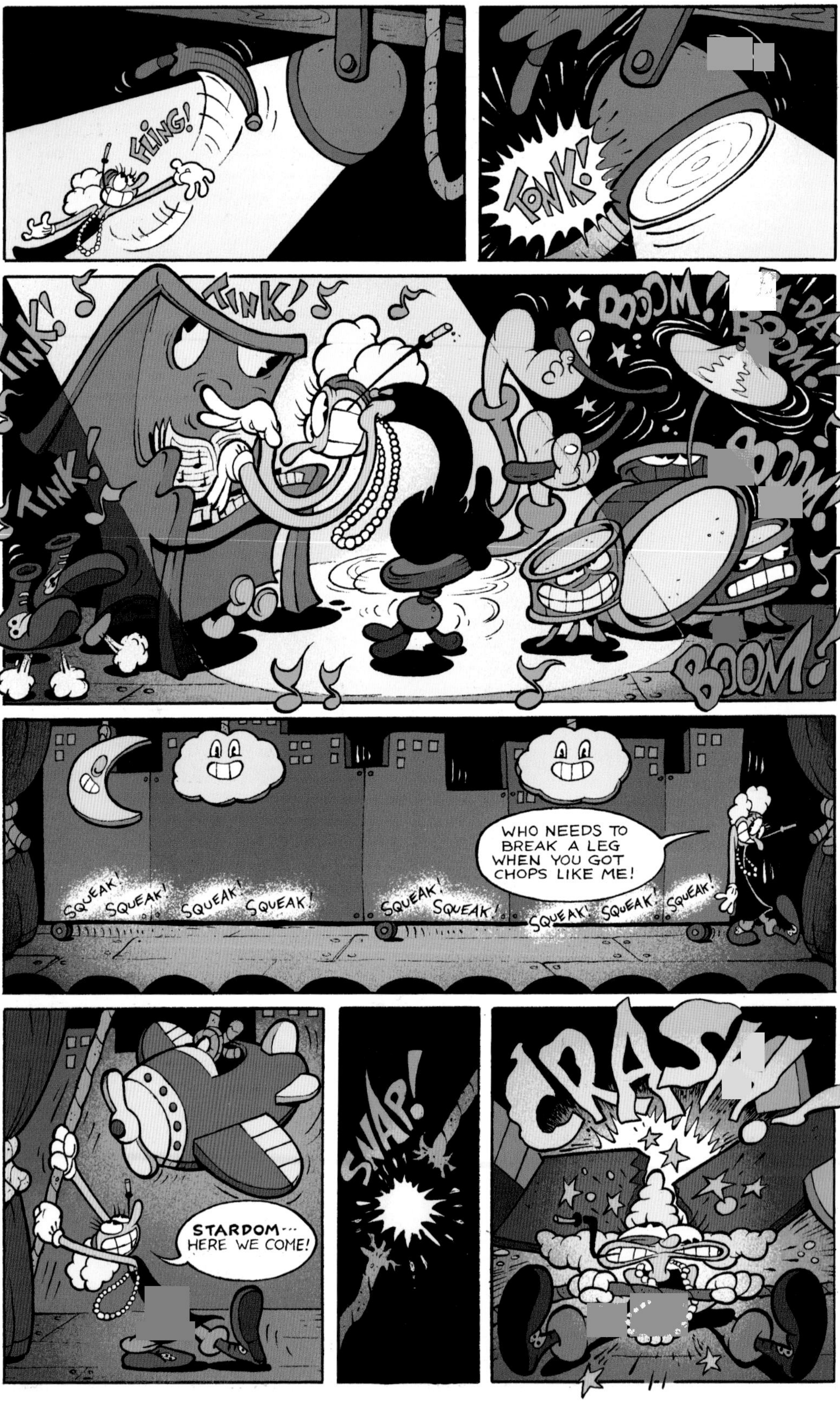
FLING!
TONK!
TINK!
TINK!
TINK!
TINK!
BOOM!
BOOM!
BOOM!
BOOM!
SQUEAK! SQUEAK! SQUEAK! SQUEAK!
SQUEAK! SQUEAK!
SQUEAK! SQUEAK! SQUEAK!
WHO NEEDS TO BREAK A LEG WHEN YOU GOT CHOPS LIKE ME!
STARDOM--- HERE WE COME!
SNAP!
CRAS

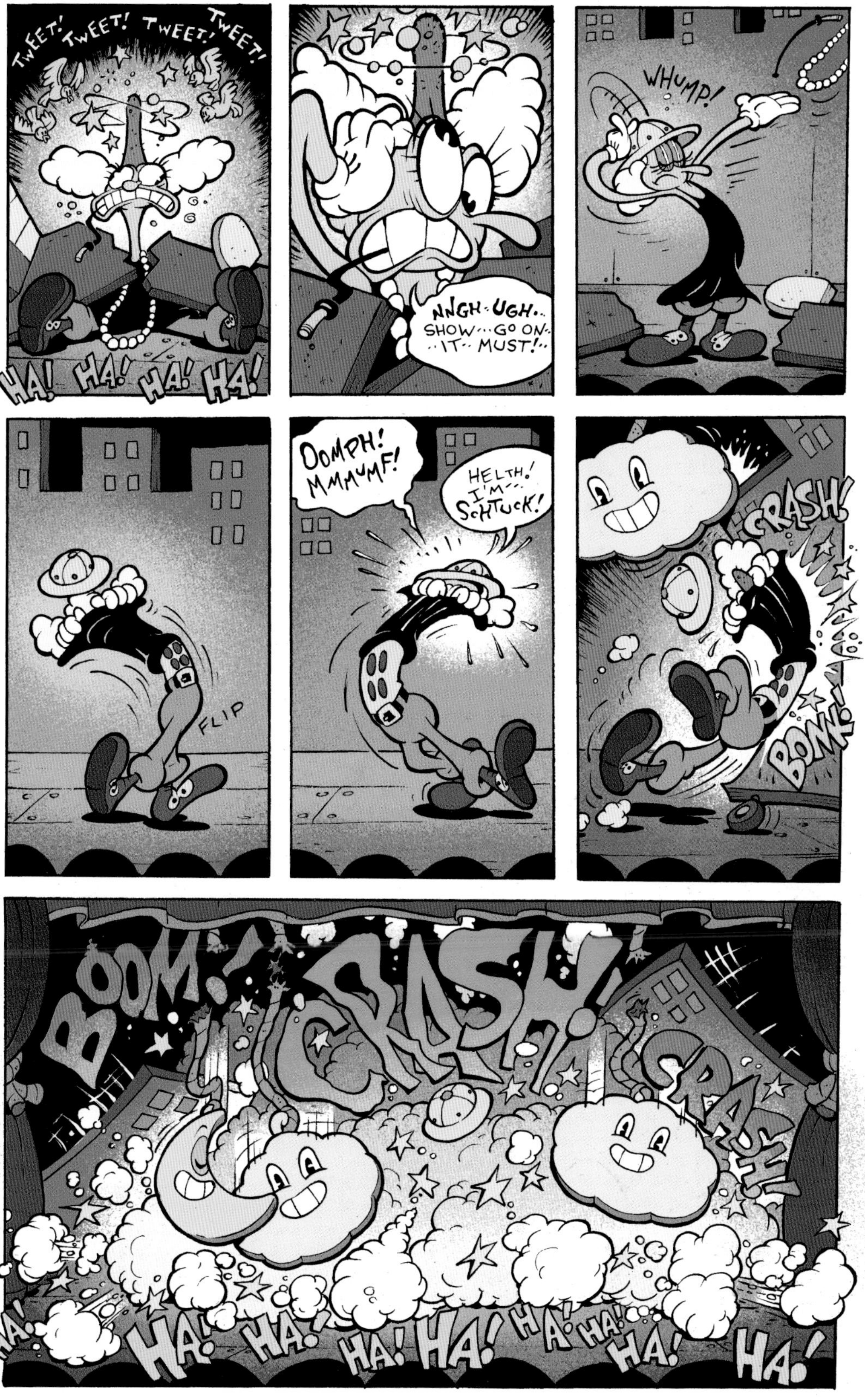
TWEET! TWEET! TWEET! TWEET!
HA! HA! HA! HA!
NNGH·UGH·· SHOW···GO ON ··IT·· MUST!··
WHUMP!
FLIP
OOMPH! MMMUMF!
HELTH! I'M·· SCHTUCK!
CRASH!
BONK!
BOOM!
CRASH!
CRASH!
HA! HA! HA! HA! HA! HA! HA! HA! HA!

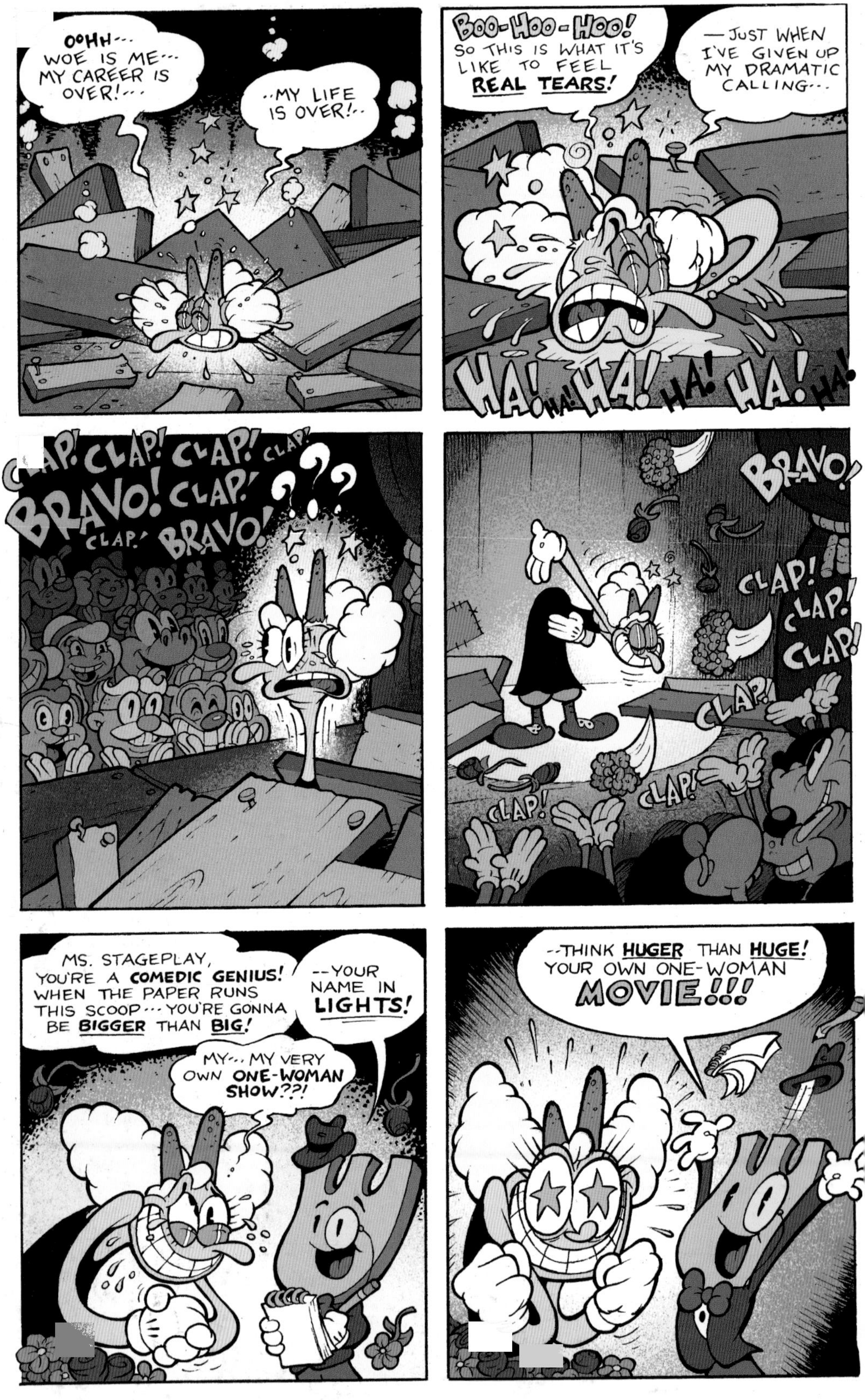
OOHH... WOE IS ME... MY CAREER IS OVER!...
...MY LIFE IS OVER!...
BOO-HOO-HOO! SO THIS IS WHAT IT'S LIKE TO FEEL REAL TEARS!
—JUST WHEN I'VE GIVEN UP MY DRAMATIC CALLING...
HA! HA! HA! HA! HA! HA!
CLAP! CLAP! CLAP! CLAP!
BRAVO! CLAP!
CLAP! BRAVO!
BRAVO!
CLAP! CLAP! CLAP!
CLAP!
CLAP!
CLAP!
MS. STAGEPLAY, YOU'RE A COMEDIC GENIUS! WHEN THE PAPER RUNS THIS SCOOP... YOU'RE GONNA BE BIGGER THAN BIG!
--YOUR NAME IN LIGHTS!
MY... MY VERY OWN ONE-WOMAN SHOW??!
--THINK HUGER THAN HUGE! YOUR OWN ONE-WOMAN MOVIE!!!

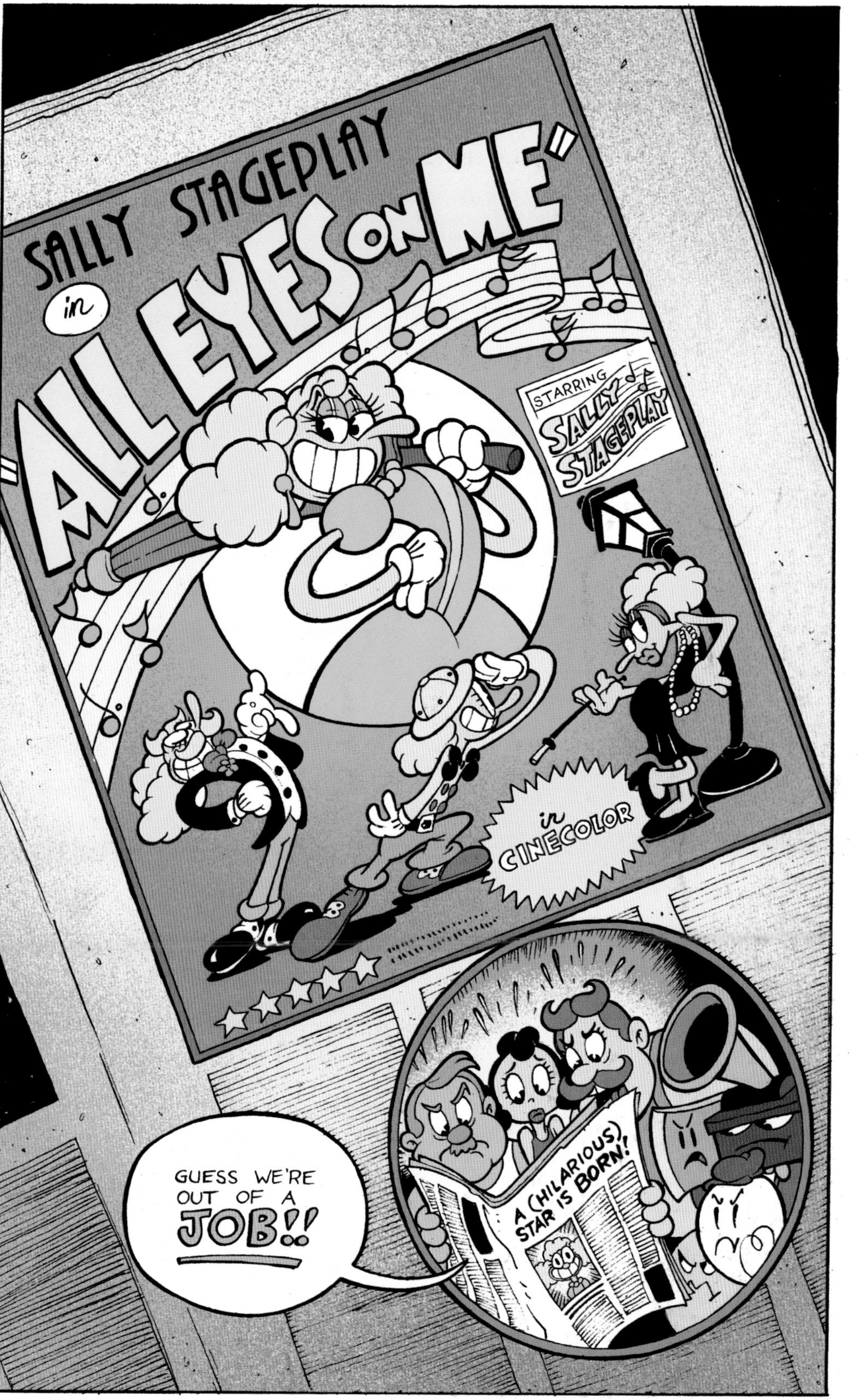

SALLY STAGEPLAY
in
"ALL EYES ON ME"
STARRING
SALLY STAGEPLAY
in
CINECOLOR
A (HILARIOUS) STAR IS BORN!
GUESS WE'RE OUT OF A JOB!!

DRAWING LESSON: THE DEVIL

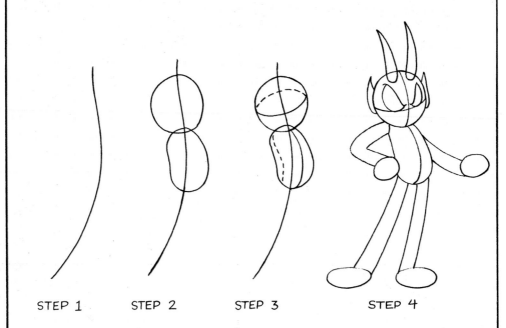

STEP 1   STEP 2   STEP 3   STEP 4

STEP 5   STEP 6

-- SHARPEN YOUR SKILLS AND MAYBE YOU CAN JOIN THE
RARIFIED—AND DID I MENTION LUCRATIVE--PROFESSION OF ARTISTE!

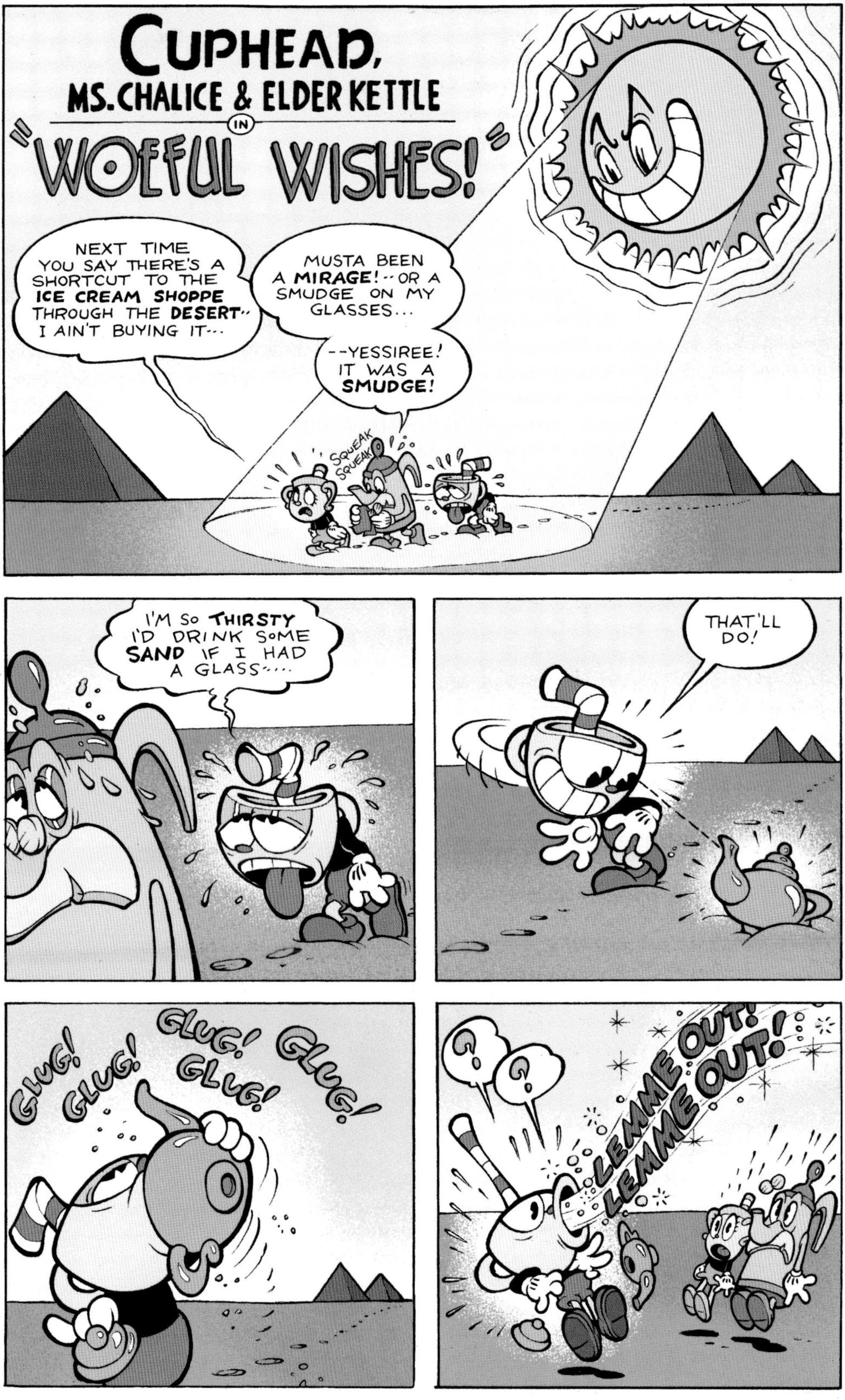
CUPHEAD,
MS. CHALICE & ELDER KETTLE
IN
"WOEFUL WISHES!"
NEXT TIME YOU SAY THERE'S A SHORTCUT TO THE ICE CREAM SHOPPE THROUGH THE DESERT.. I AIN'T BUYING IT...
MUSTA BEEN A MIRAGE! --OR A SMUDGE ON MY GLASSES...
--YESSIREE! IT WAS A SMUDGE!
SQUEAK SQUEAK
I'M SO THIRSTY I'D DRINK SOME SAND IF I HAD A GLASS....
THAT'LL DO!
GLUG! GLUG! GLUG! GLUG! GLUG!
LEMME OUT! LEMME OUT!

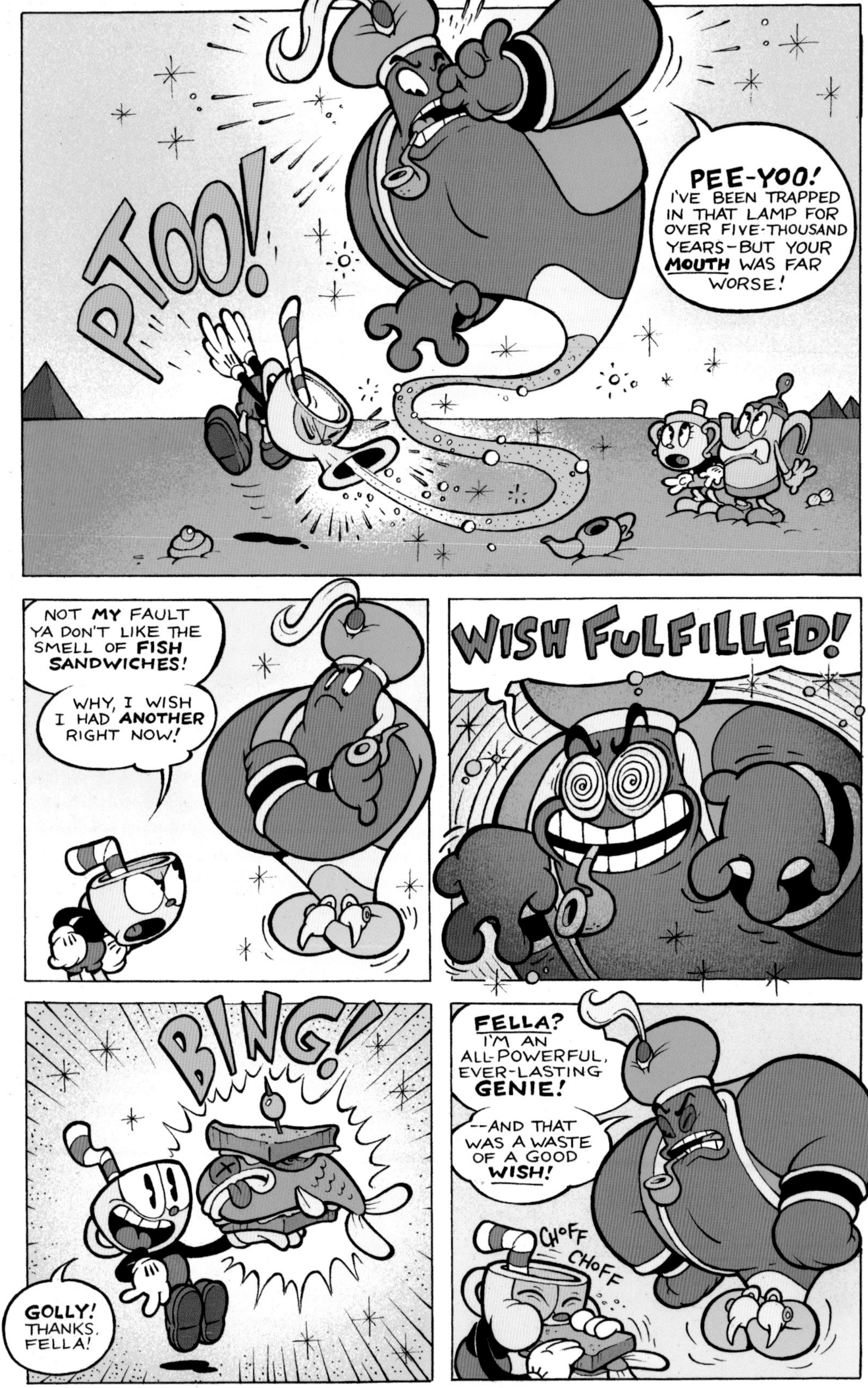
PTOO!
PEE-YOO! I'VE BEEN TRAPPED IN THAT LAMP FOR OVER FIVE-THOUSAND YEARS—BUT YOUR MOUTH WAS FAR WORSE!
NOT MY FAULT YA DON'T LIKE THE SMELL OF FISH SANDWICHES!
WHY, I WISH I HAD ANOTHER RIGHT NOW!
WISH FULFILLED!
BING!
GOLLY! THANKS, FELLA!
FELLA? I'M AN ALL-POWERFUL, EVER-LASTING GENIE!
--AND THAT WAS A WASTE OF A GOOD WISH!
CHOFF
CHOFF

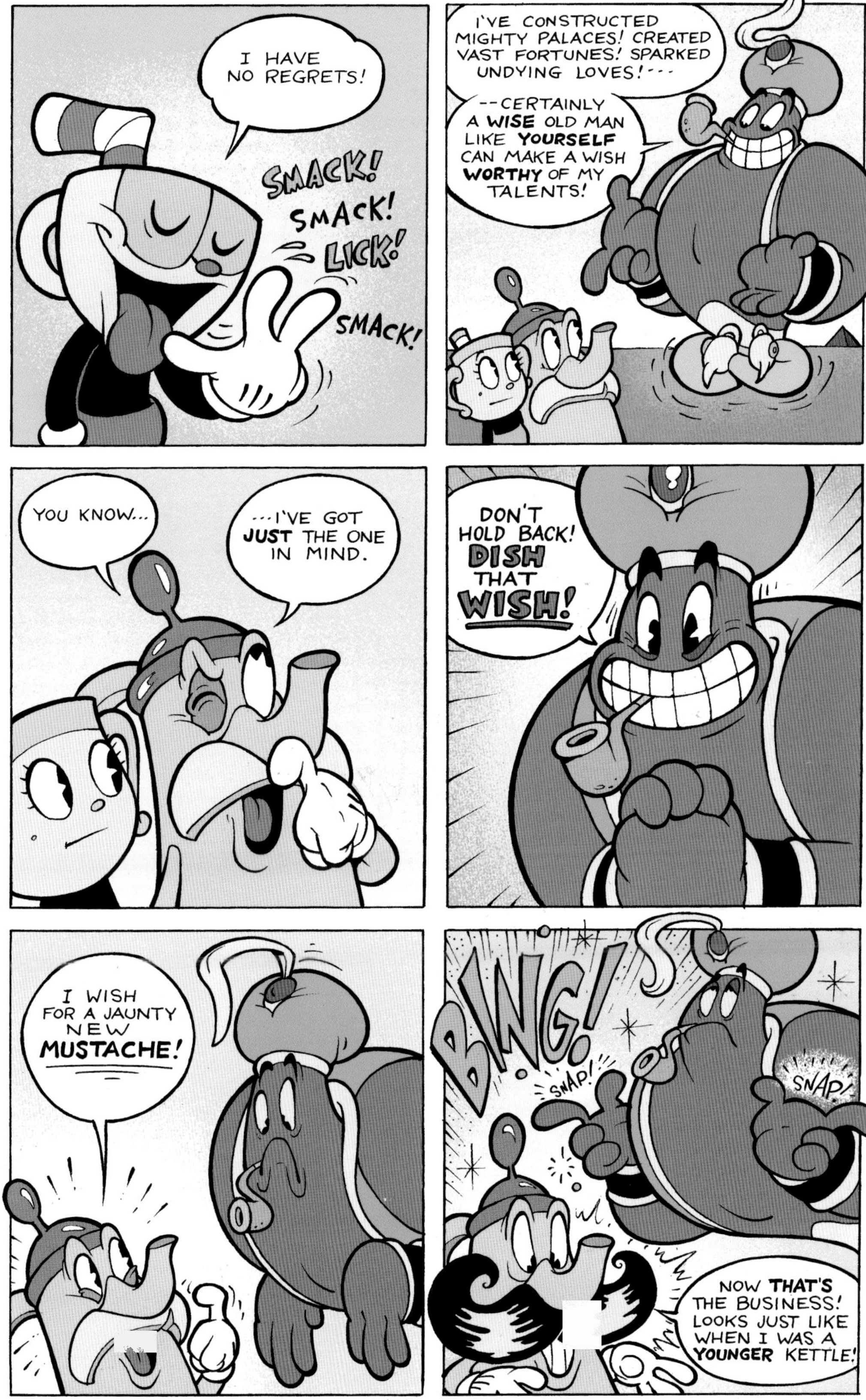
I HAVE NO REGRETS!
SMACK!
SMACK!
LICK!
SMACK!
I'VE CONSTRUCTED MIGHTY PALACES! CREATED VAST FORTUNES! SPARKED UNDYING LOVES!---
--CERTAINLY A WISE OLD MAN LIKE YOURSELF CAN MAKE A WISH WORTHY OF MY TALENTS!
YOU KNOW...
...I'VE GOT JUST THE ONE IN MIND.
DON'T HOLD BACK! DISH THAT WISH!
I WISH FOR A JAUNTY NEW MUSTACHE!
BING!
SNAP!
SNAP!
NOW THAT'S THE BUSINESS! LOOKS JUST LIKE WHEN I WAS A YOUNGER KETTLE!

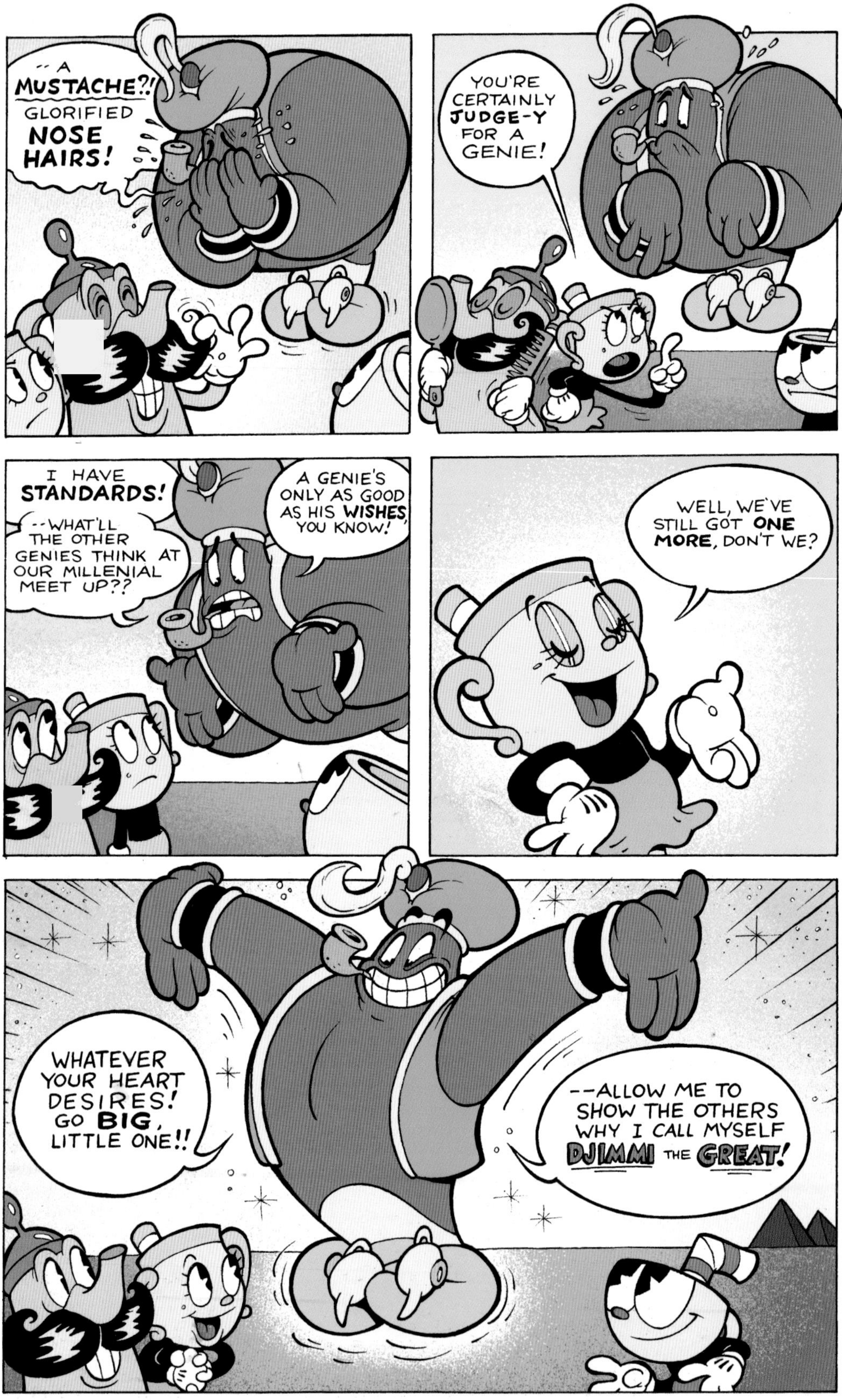
--A MUSTACHE?!
GLORIFIED NOSE HAIRS!
YOU'RE CERTAINLY JUDGE-Y FOR A GENIE!
I HAVE STANDARDS!
--WHAT'LL THE OTHER GENIES THINK AT OUR MILLENIAL MEET UP??
A GENIE'S ONLY AS GOOD AS HIS WISHES, YOU KNOW!
WELL, WE'VE STILL GOT ONE MORE, DON'T WE?
WHATEVER YOUR HEART DESIRES! GO BIG, LITTLE ONE!!
--ALLOW ME TO SHOW THE OTHERS WHY I CALL MYSELF DJIMMI THE GREAT!

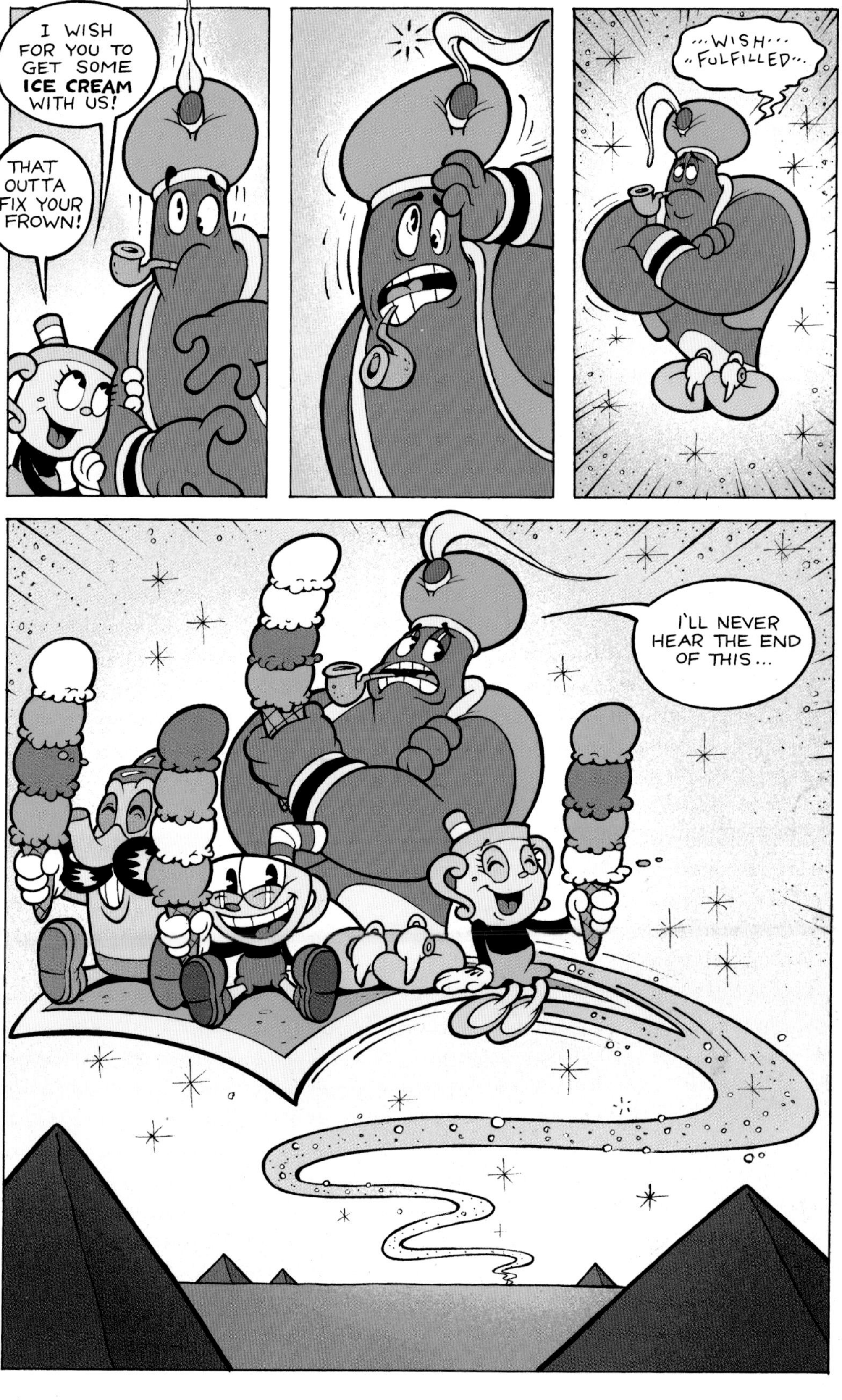
I WISH FOR YOU TO GET SOME **ICE CREAM** WITH US!
THAT OUTTA FIX YOUR FROWN!
...WISH... ...FULFILLED...
I'LL NEVER HEAR THE END OF THIS...

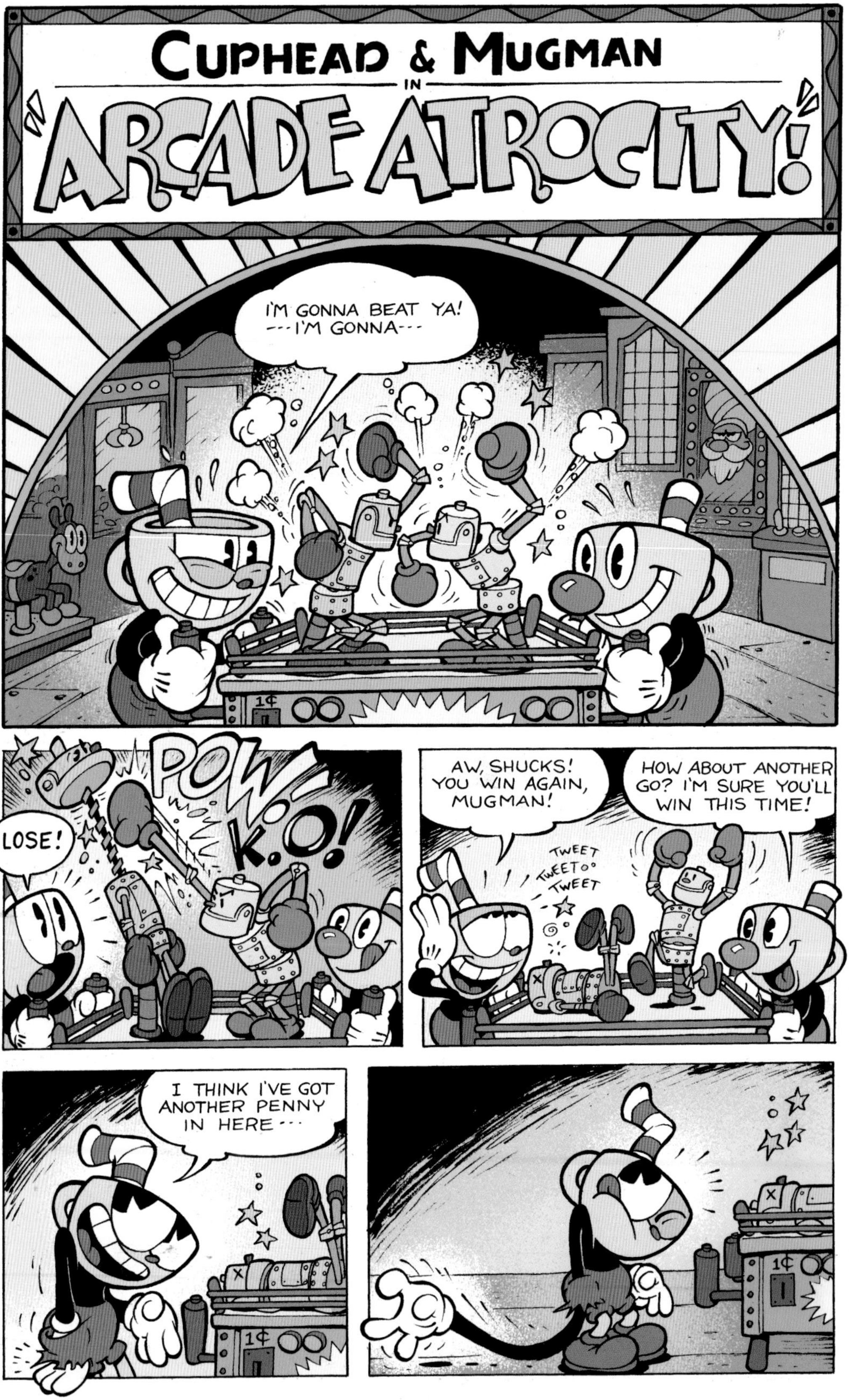
CUPHEAD & MUGMAN
IN
"ARCADE ATROCITY!"
I'M GONNA BEAT YA! ---I'M GONNA---
1¢
POW
K.O!
LOSE!
AW, SHUCKS! YOU WIN AGAIN, MUGMAN!
HOW ABOUT ANOTHER GO? I'M SURE YOU'LL WIN THIS TIME!
TWEET TWEET TWEET
I THINK I'VE GOT ANOTHER PENNY IN HERE---
1¢
1¢

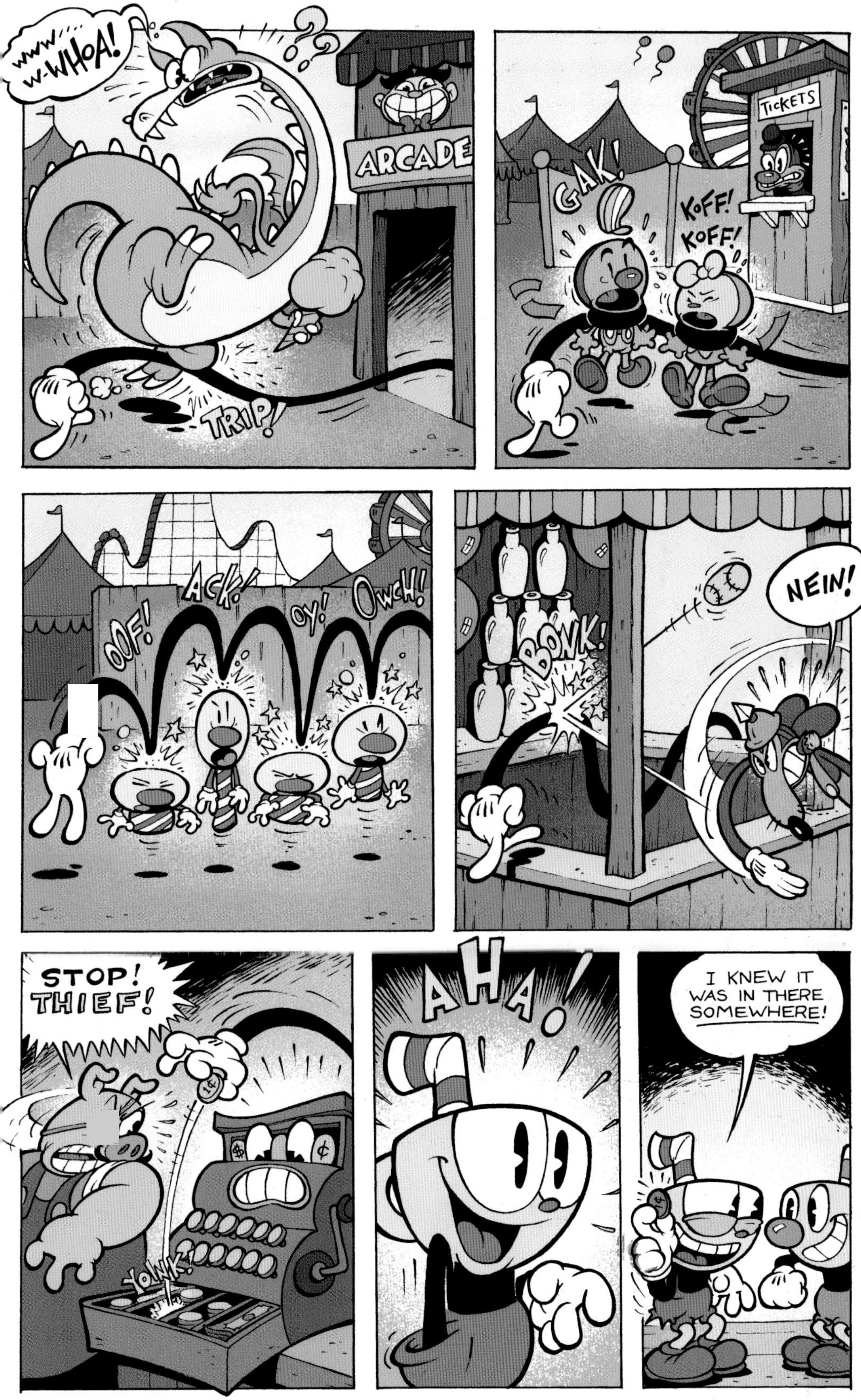
WWW.... W-WHOA!
ARCADE
TRIP!
TICKETS
GAK!
KOFF! KOFF!
OOF!
ACK!
OY!
OWCH!
BONK!
NEIN!
STOP! THIEF!
YOINK!
AHA!
I KNEW IT WAS IN THERE SOMEWHERE!

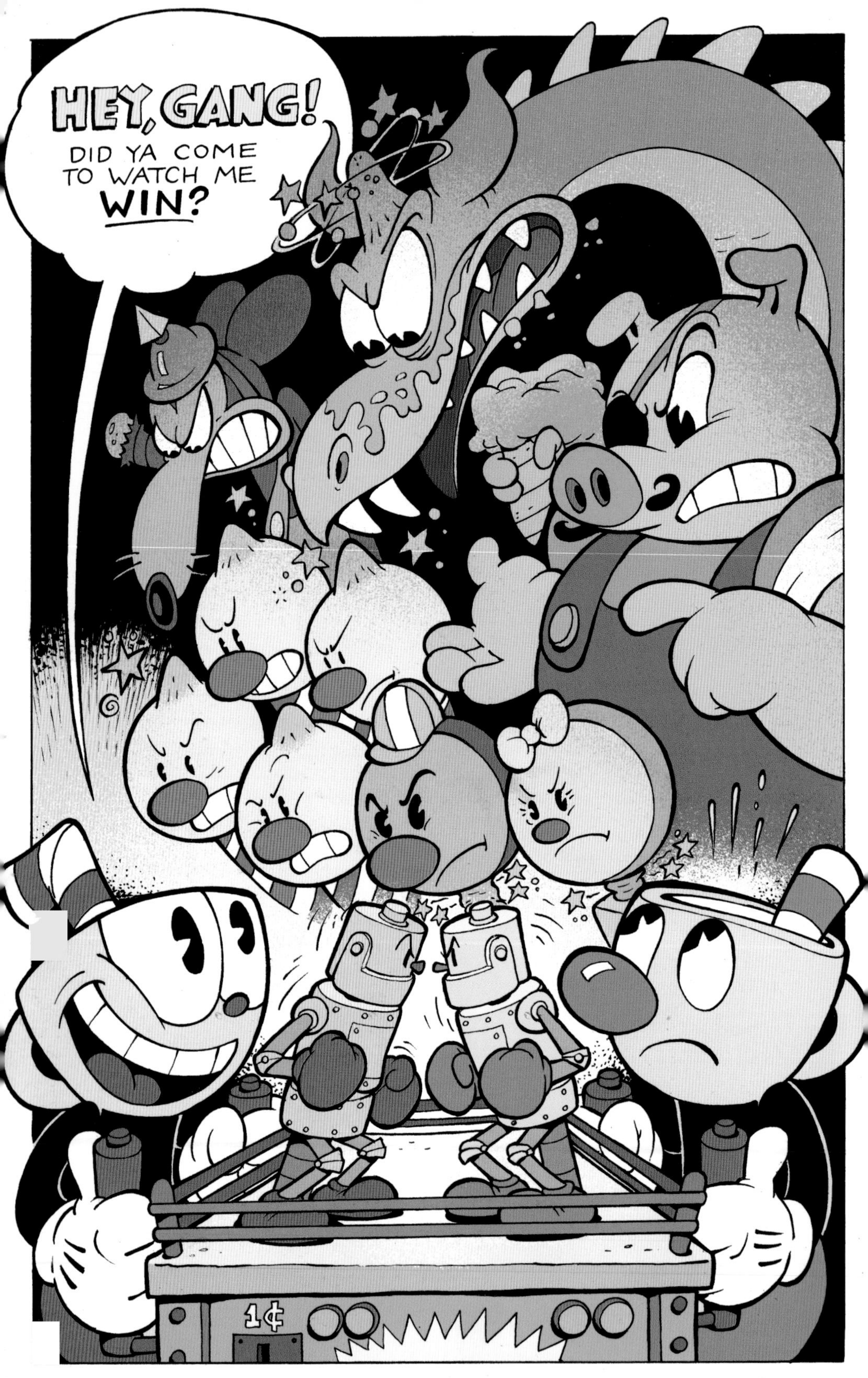
HEY, GANG! DID YA COME TO WATCH ME WIN?
1¢

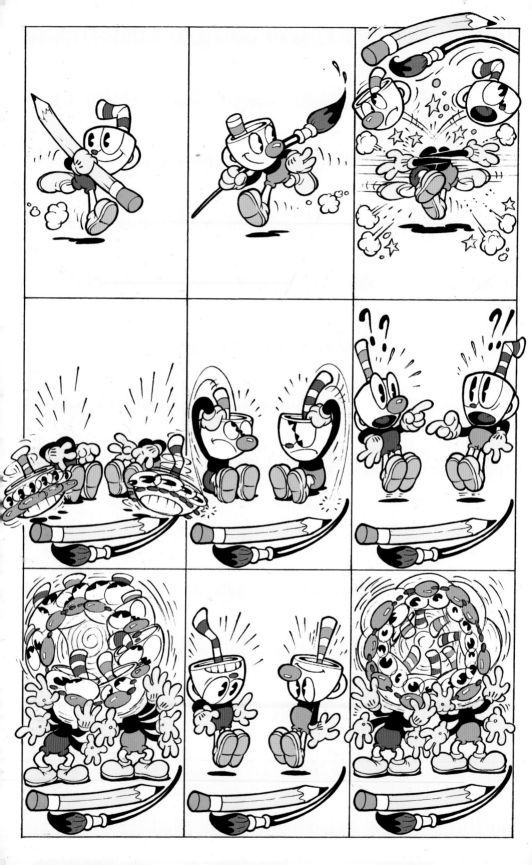

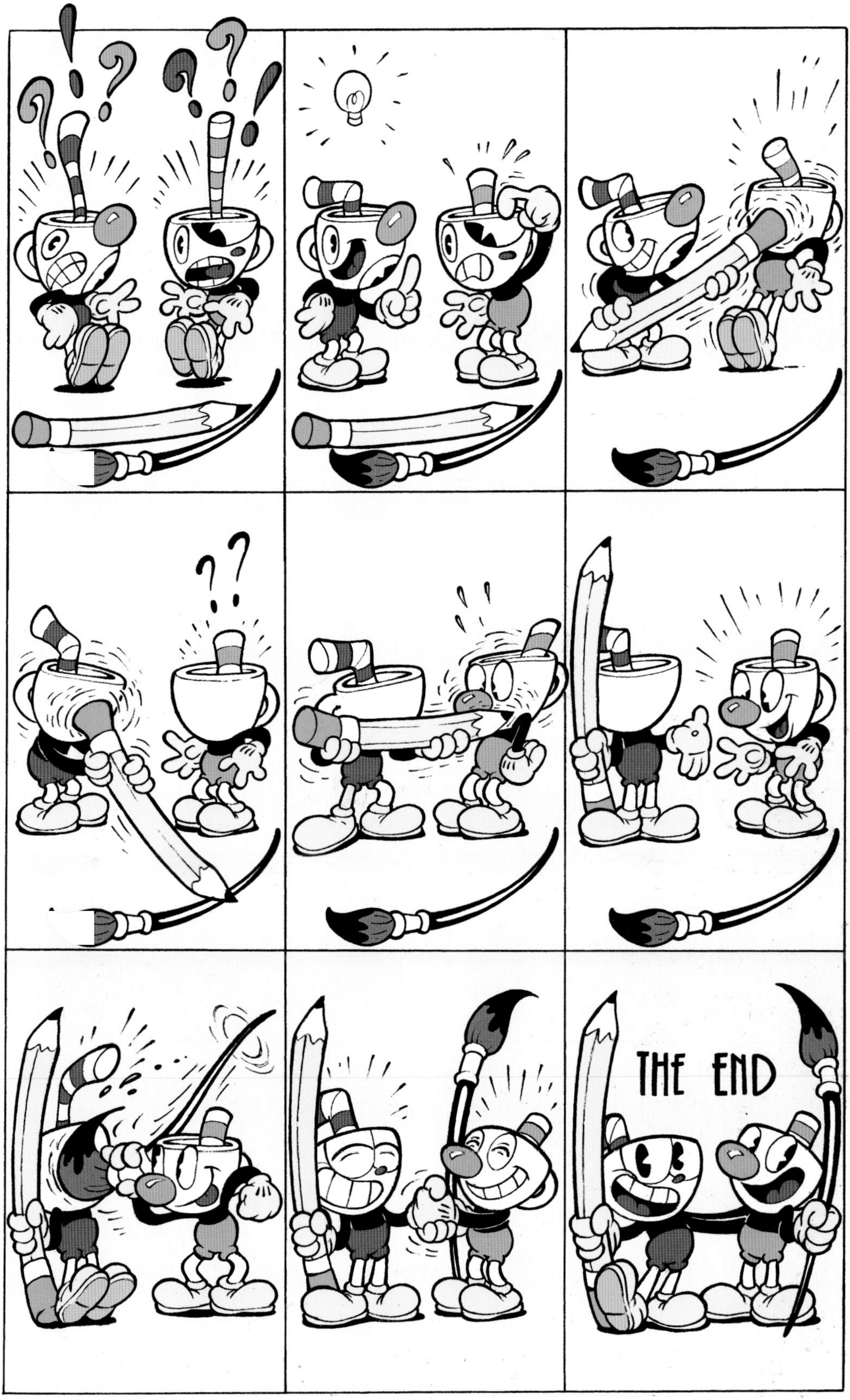
THE END